DOUBLE FUDGE FELONY

BOOK THREE IN THE CUPCAKE CRIMES SERIES

MOLLY MAPLE

D1739317

MARY E. TWOMEY LLC

DOUBLE FUDGE FELONY

Book Three in the Cupcake Crimes Series

By

Molly Maple

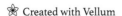 Created with Vellum

To the people who bring out the best in me.
You each deserve a cupcake.

ABOUT DOUBLE FUDGE FELONY

When Charlotte McKay's new friend is accused of murder, she will do anything to solve the crime.

When Charlotte befriends Lisa Swanson, her dreams of owning a cupcake bakery finally begin to come true. But when a body is discovered and all signs point to Lisa being the guilty one, Charlotte doesn't know what to believe.

Murder isn't the only crime that Charlotte uncovers in her quest to clear Lisa's name. When secret sins come to light, soon the plucky citizens in the small town of Sweetwater Falls don't seem quite so innocent anymore.

"Double Fudge Felony" is filled with layered clues and cozy moments, written by Molly Maple, which is a pen name for a USA Today bestselling author.

BROWN SNOWBALL FIGHT

*A*unt Winifred is no stranger to a hard day's work, but after a week like we've had, I'm not sure even her determined vigor has enough pep left to finish the job.

She swats a fly from the curly silver hair that kisses her shoulders, frowning at the pest for bothering her when she's already agitated. "Whose bright idea was it to have the Farmer's Fair at Ben's farm?"

Marianne snickers. My best friend sets her rake down and stretches her back. Her dainty hands raise above her head while she twists at the waist. "That's not the real question. The thing I want to know is why on earth did we sign up to help with cleanup duties? We had to know that an event that features pony rides and feeding sheep would mean a wheelbarrow full of animal poop." Her olive skin is sun-kissed today, making her naturally lovely complexion glow.

Agnes massages a crick in her neck. "Charlotte McKay, you should have talked us out of signing up for this. If only there had been a sign-up for baking cupcakes to pass out. You could have done the baking and we could have handed them out. Perfection."

It's my dream to open up a cupcake shop. If there had been a slot for donating baked goods, I would have jumped on the opportunity.

I take Agnes' scolding with a smile and a slight chuckle. "Oh, sure. Let's blame it on me. I suggested we sign up to help with the pony rides. I was outvoted because Marianne gets spooked by horses."

Marianne's neck shrinks. "I didn't realize this was the only other option."

Aunt Winifred stabs at the hay with her shovel. "I say we leave the manure where it sits and let it fertilize the field." Her expression lifts. "I really like that idea, come to think of it."

I take the wheelbarrow with both hands, wincing at the sting of my blisters through the work gloves. "Farmer Ben agreed to let Sweetwater Falls use his field for the Farmer's Fair if afterward the manure was moved to his vegetable garden. Can't back out now. He held up his end of the bargain. The petting zoo was a success. The city raised over a thousand dollars to help rebuild the fountain in the park."

Aunt Winifred groans dramatically. "I'm not twenty-eight, like you, honey cake. I'm too old to be shoveling and whatnot. This silver hair isn't just for show."

Karen Newby hisses from her lawn chair a few yards away. "Bite your tongue, Winnie! We are not too old for anything." She takes a sip of her lemonade, rubbing it in that she didn't sign up for cleanup duty. I'm fairly certain she only came to gloat. Though, she's so tiny, I'm glad she's not expected to wield a wheelbarrow. She grins at us, her dentures a hair too wide for her thin and wiry face.

Agnes wipes sweat from her brow, looking just as displeased that we signed up for this job as the rest of us. But her measured and pleasant personality takes over, as it always does. "Lots of out of towners at the event yesterday. It was nice seeing so many new faces." She swats a fly away from her short white curls that have been pinned away from her rounded face.

Aunt Winifred has been doing little more than stabbing at the hay for the past ten minutes. Being that she is well past the age of being able to shovel for an hour straight, Marianne and I make it our business to pick up the slack.

"You missed a spot," Karen calls from her lawn chair. The elderly waif of a woman wouldn't look quite so ridiculous if she wasn't holding her drink in one hand, and a book in the other.

Marianne and I merely shoot Karen derisive giggles, but Agnes puts her hands on her generous hips, gearing up to set Karen straight. "We missed a spot, did we? Care to come help us?"

"I didn't sign up for the cleanup crew, I'll remind you. I'll also point out that I warned all four of you ladies that volunteering for this would be a bad idea. I did my duty for Sweetwater Falls. I passed out scoops of animal food to the children who wanted to feed the sheep."

Winifred snickers at the disparate amount of effort required between Karen's task and ours. "Fine, fine. We should have listened to you. But you didn't have to come out here to revel in our misery."

Karen leans back in her chair, fanning herself dramatically with her book. "Who says I'm reveling? I wanted to do some sunbathing, and you all coincidentally happened to be working in the place where I'm getting my much-needed Vitamin D."

I narrow one eye at Karen, though my reply is lighthearted. "Hard to sunbathe with long sleeves and a hat with a giant brim all the way around."

Karen bats her eyelashes in my direction. "I'm working my way up to taking my hat off. You all have such interesting hairdos today. I don't want to upstage you. Might hurt morale."

Aunt Winifred, Karen and Agnes are best friends, and the

founders of the very exclusive Live Forever Club. They're always together, always up to something fun.

Except for today, when two-thirds of them are shoveling manure with my best friend and me.

Agnes groans at Karen's humor. "You know what's wrong with this manure? What's making it so hard to scoop up?"

"What?" Marianne asks, swooshing one of her two chocolate-colored braids over her shoulder.

"It's not sticky enough in this section. Some of it dried out overnight. If we'd cleaned up right when the festival ended at sundown, we might have had a fighting chance. But see," Agnes pauses and bends toward the dirt. One of her curls has come loose and tickles her neck. "See, this is too dry." She stands, revealing a fistful of animal poop.

Marianne grimaces. "Agnes, gross. Put it down."

Agnes shrugs. "What? I'm wearing gloves. Unlike some people who didn't dress for the occasion." A wicked grin spreads across her pink-painted mouth. "Karen, what do you think of the consistency?"

Instead of opening her palm to display the manure to Karen, who is seated several yards away, Agnus winds up and launches the ball of poop at her best friend.

I had no idea Agnes was such a good shot. Marianne and Karen shriek in unison when the manure hits Karen's shoulder and feathers apart on impact.

My mouth drops open as Agnes lets out a loud, joyful belly laugh that rings across the empty field. "Ho! That was priceless. It's been a while since I've thrown a softball, but I guess it's like riding a bike."

I'm sure most people in Karen's position would be horrified. They might run back to their car and drive to the nearest shower to scrub the filth off themselves. But Karen's grin stretches from ear to ear as she stands. "*Now* it's a party!"

With no work gloves on, Karen reaches down with her bony fingers and scoops up a handful of manure. Gotta love the thick stomach of a grown woman.

It's Aunt Winifred's turn to yelp when Karen's subpar aim sends the poop hurtling past Agnes straight onto Winifred's shirt. Winifred's face pulls at the mess. "You're lucky I borrowed this shirt, or I'd be fixing to take you down, Karen."

"You borrowed it from me!" Karen laughs, picking up another handful as Agnes does the same.

"Hey, that's right. Well, then fire away!" Winifred grins, doing a little shimmy to draw more manure her way. She laughs as she joins in the fight, lobbing a ball of feces at the back of Agnes' head.

Marianne squeals as she drops her rake and runs toward me. "I am not going down like this! You three are nuts!"

"Come on!" Agnes shouts after her protégé. "You haven't lived until you've had a brown snowball fight."

"Gross! You're crazy!" Marianne's sprint away from the jovial brawl is an open invitation for Karen to lob a smattering of manure at her back. Of course, Karen's aim is dreadful, so the poop smacks on my chest and splinters out over my ribcage.

I shudder through my grimace. This is no time to be holding back on the theatrics. I've seen some horrible things since I've moved to Sweetwater Falls a few months ago. I discovered Amos' body when he'd been dead for a couple of days. I also witnessed Gerald Forbine's state of decomposition when I found his body atop a compost pile.

But in all my life, I have never had the misfortune of wearing sheep and horse poop smeared across my shirt.

"Karen, we aren't in the fight!" I protest, though waiving my arms to forbid another assault is somehow seen as an invitation to throw yet more feces my way.

Aunt Winnie giggles. "I'm curious to know what that golden

blonde hair of yours would look like if it was brown. Fancy being a brunette for the day, Charlotte McKay?" she rhymes.

I cover my hair with my hands. "Ack! Don't you dare!"

Agnes laughs as she nails Marianne in the hip. My best friend is cowering to my side now, her slender frame huddled to my taller stature, making me the more obvious target. Agnes scoops up another handful, eyeing us with intention. "Do you remember your nickname?"

I know mine. My name from the Live Forever Club is Charlotte the Brave—quite the ironic label most days.

Marianne's mousy reply is laughable. "Marianne the Wild?" She says it like a question, like my sweet little librarian would never dream of being associated with that particular adjective.

Agnes molds the poop into a ball-shape. "That's right! When you don't like what life's been throwing at you, what do you do? Do you run away?"

Before Marianne can answer, Winnie cheers a hearty "No!" with her fist in the air.

"Marianne," I warn her, a smile sneaking over my face as I finally decide to give in to the chaos.

She shakes her head, her brown braids swinging in time with her fear. "Don't you dare. If we don't participate, eventually they'll run out of energy." She looks like a cartoon princess rife with worry. Her voice is even higher pitched, adding to the inherent innocence of her demeanor.

How she ever took up with the wild ladies of the Live Forever Club, I'll never know.

But I sure am grateful she brought me along for the ride. I love these crazy ladies.

I chuckle at Marianne's logic. "You've met the Live Forever Club, right? Their energy will outlast ours every single time. Best be wild. Do you want to get old someday and have to say to your grandchildren that you've never had a brown snowball fight?"

"Yes!" Marianne squeaks. "That's exactly what I want to say!"

I fix her with a mischievous grin. "Well, it's too late for that, you wild woman." Marianne whimpers as I bend down to pick up a handful of the muck.

My aim doesn't need to be perfect to hit my great Aunt Winifred square in the shoulder. The slurpy sound of the slop hitting her shirt is satisfying in a way I didn't anticipate. I hoot and clap for my good shot, cheering myself on because that is exactly the sort of confidence this situation calls for.

Though Karen isn't fast by any means, she jogs after us, aiming to take us both down with a single shot.

I squeal and run while Marianne surprises us all and stands her ground. I glance over my shoulder, watching with wonder and horror as Marianne picks up the smallest amount of manure she can form into a squishy ball. A cheer erupts from both Agnes and myself when Marianne launches the poop at Karen. There's a manic gleam in her eyes that does make her truly look wild.

I love it. Marianne is such a controlled, tightly wound person. To witness one of her rare moments of letting go, even though I'm watching over my shoulder as I run away, is a thing of greatness. I love her so much.

I love her even more when she jumps up and down, waving her hands in front of her face. "I did it! That's so disgusting! Karen, I..."

But Karen lobs a handful at Marianne before Marianne can truly revel in her victory.

I make to turn my head back to look where I'm running, but it's too late. My muddy shoe (I really hope it's mud) catches on something firm I'm not expecting to run across. My body hurdles over the object, and I land with a thud on all fours. "Oh!"

"You alright, Charlotte?" Aunt Winnie calls after me.

"Yeah. I just tripped over this..." But when I roll to sit upright, it isn't an errant log I see in the field. My mouth falls open at the long body sprawled out, its eyes staring straight back at me, frozen in horror.

My mouth opens to scream, but no sound comes out. Apparently I spent all my volume on the brown snowball fight. The sight of the dead man before me renders me completely mute. *"Marianne!"* I mouth, but there's still no sound.

Karen and Marianne are elbow-deep in a one-on-one manure match, so they don't notice my panic. It's Aunt Winifred who trots over to me, a long smear of poop streaked down the side of her face. "Honey cake, what's wrong?"

But I don't have the words to respond. I don't know how to say that I just found a body. Instead, I fumble with my pocket, tugging out my phone and getting manure on the device. I snap a picture of a well-built man perhaps in his young thirties who is wearing a striped polo and designer jeans.

I may live in a small town now, but I'm from Chicago and know expensive clothing when I see it. His feet are splayed unnaturally, his mouth open in a frozen scream that no one heard.

A fun day at the Farmer's Fair ended in death for one very unfortunate man.

2

STALLION AND SWAN

The five of us shift uncomfortably from side to side as we stand in the field. We answer Sheriff Flowers' questions, though we don't have much more information than he can gather by looking at the dead body himself. Sheriff Flowers already checked the pockets for a wallet, but they turned up empty.

So it could have been a robbery gone wrong.

"I'm guessing putting you ladies in charge of the cleanup wasn't the brightest idea," Sheriff Flowers comments, motioning to our manure-stained apparel.

Karen lifts her chin. "We stumbled upon a crime, so it evens out, having us here." She looks down at her pink pants and white shirt, which are stained beyond repair. "And I happen to think we did a fantastic job of cleaning up. We're wearing most of the manure that was left on the ground."

Sheriff Flowers snorts and takes out his tiny notepad.

My focus is tethered to the man in the grass, still sprawled out with no name and no obvious killer in sight. Poor guy. Went to a petting zoo and met his end after feeding a few lambs.

The man has bruising around his neck, which tells me he

didn't meet his doom choking on a carnival hot dog. "I don't recognize him," I reply when Sheriff Flowers asks me if I've seen this man before. I'm not the best person to weigh in, though, as I've only lived in Sweetwater Falls for a few months.

Marianne's answer is much the same as mine, but Agnes pauses, tilting her head to the side to get a better look at the man.

He's lying supine, his legs sprawled. His eyes and mouth are open with a silent scream frozen on his face. His tan hair is combed to the side, though sticking up in parts.

Agnes' voice is quiet, but it still carries to the rest of us. "Winifred, does he sort of look like the man who..." She pauses and gives Winifred a look that tells me she's holding back from saying something scandalous. Agnes jerks her chin toward the body, fixing her eyes on Aunt Winnie. "You know. Lisa Swanson's..." She raises her eyebrows twice.

Now I *have* to know who this guy is, and what he's done that could seal Agnes' lips like that. "Lisa Swanson's what?" I ask, not willing to be cut out of the reveal just because I'm new in town, and Agnes is afraid I might have delicate ears.

Great Aunt Winifred gasps, her hand fluttering over her heart. "Oh, no." She looks up at Sheriff Flowers. "Agnes might be right. This young man looks like Lisa Swanson's personal trainer. I only saw him in passing a few times, but I think this is him."

Sheriff Flowers jots down a few words in his notepad. "Does the fella have a name?"

Agnes grimaces, looking from Karen to Winifred for help. "Young Stallion? That's what Delia calls him. No idea what his actual name is."

Karen leans over to get a closer look at the body. "If you want to know everything about this man, your first stop will need to be Lisa Swanson. Might want to wait to talk to her until her husband is at work. Don't want to pop poor Wesley's bubble. He's still in denial about her affair."

Aunt Winnie throws her head back. "Still? I thought Delia said Wesley caught her having an affair. Caught her in the act."

Agnes clucks her tongue and shakes her head. "Denial goes a long way when you're in love. Poor Wesley."

Marianne's face pulls. "His company is the one I hired to fix the leaky roof of the library. I see him just about every day. Oh, he'll know that I know!"

Marianne recently inherited a small fortune with the stipulations that it must be spent to fund the library, where she works as the head librarian. The first thing she did with the money was make a list and set to fixing all the things that were in dire need of repair. She hired all local contractors, so the money would benefit the businesses of Sweetwater Falls.

Marianne is the sweetest person on the planet. I am certain that when she sees Wesley next, she won't be able to hold herself together, knowing a secret this big that might crush him.

The sound of an engine distracts me from the dead body. When a navy pickup comes into view, I feel the blood drain from my face.

"Oh, look who it is, Charlotte!" Aunt Winifred sings, elbowing me in the side.

"Can I go?" I borderline beg the sheriff. "Like, can this be done? You can take it from here, right?"

He glances toward the truck, which parks a stone's throw away. "You got a problem with my son?"

The urge to vomit occurs to my stomach. "No! Of course not. Logan is…"

Even saying his name is too much.

Marianne giggles at how flustered I get around him. "Logan is pretty." Marianne fills in the rest of my sentence for the sheriff.

If I could vanish into thin air, that would solve it all.

The sheriff's head snaps toward me, surprised that this is the reason I want to run away. As if it's strange anyone finds his son to be the handsomest man that has ever walked the earth.

Though Marianne is still upset about the murder, her favorite show is the Charlotte and Logan Comedy Hour. Every time I get near the man, I make a clumsy fool of myself. I either break something or trip over my own two feet. It's the worst. Logan is too handsome. He's too good looking to be near, yet every now and then, I find myself in close proximity to his neatly trimmed honey-colored hair and dimpled smile. He has high cheekbones and a jaw so angular it could cut glass. His shoulders are broad and his waist is narrow.

Combine that with a police uniform, and I'm done for.

One day I hope I will get over my crush, but as Logan walks toward us with a small smile aimed my way, I know that day is not today. He dips his head toward the five of us. "Good morning, Ladies. What sort of mischief did you find for yourselves today?" He motions to our poop-smeared attire.

Why a lightning bolt doesn't shoot down from the sky to save me from this moment, I'll never know. If I ran into Logan wearing my very best outfit, I would still be embarrassed because he is so spectacularly stunning. To see him when I'm sweaty and covered in manure, standing a couple feet away from a dead body?

This is not my finest moment.

I motion to the man on the ground. "We found the stallion and then the poop throwing." I shake my head. "No, the poop came first. Then the stallion. But he's dead. And then Swans."

Sheriff Flowers stares at me as if I've gone insane while Marianne bursts into fits of giggles. "The poop throwing! I love it. Oh, that is the best sum-up any of us could give. Well done, Charlotte." She claps her hands, earning the stink eye from me.

Logan knows all about my crush. He's so kind that he took

pity on me and occasionally came over to hang out with Marianne and me when I was baking regularly. Now that I don't have a baking gig anymore, I haven't seen him in a couple of weeks.

I'd hoped that my crush would have died down, but it seems it's only gotten worse.

Logan's mouth draws to the side. "Dad, you want to fill me in? What's this about a horse and swans?"

Great Aunt Winifred chimes in, explaining the story in greater detail to Logan. "We signed up to do cleanup after the fair. While we were working, my beautiful, single, talented grandniece stumbled across this poor fella, already dead." My neck shrinks at her praise, but she breezes on. "We think it might be the Young Stallion Lisa Swanson is rumored to have taken up with."

Agnes leans in, her eyebrows bouncing twice. "Lisa's personal trainer."

Logan closes his eyes and nods. "That's terrible."

"Should we go?" I ask the girls, sounding a little too chipper, given that we're in the presence of a dead body. "We should go. The yikes with the clothes and the murder and the affair. To the... we should go to go."

Marianne snickers. "Smooth."

"Not so fast, ladies." Sheriff Flowers eyes Aunt Winnie, then casts a look of suspicion onto the other two members of the Live Forever Club. "Funny that you all discovered the dead body out here. The carnival was packed. Odd that no one saw the body then."

I guess it is strange. That must mean that Young Stallion was murdered after the fair ended and the animals were put back in their stables. That would put the time of death anywhere between eight o'clock last night and ten o'clock this morning. We could have started the job earlier, but I had a terrible time getting Aunt Winnie out the door. For some reason she didn't want to clean up poop all afternoon.

Poor Young Stallion, dead for hours and all alone.

I really need to learn this guy's name.

Sheriff Flowers has a different opinion. "Funny that you just so happen to be the only ones to find the body. It's a good place for a body dump, if you ask me. No one around."

Karen's chest puffs as she takes a step toward the sheriff. He's in his sixties and stands a couple inches taller than my proud five-foot-ten, but he looks smaller when the frail and tiny Karen confronts him. "What are you suggesting, Louis?"

He blanches, his chin dimple deepening. He brushes his fingers through his salt-and-pepper hair, trying to maintain his composure. "I know how you ladies like to stick together. I won't get a confession out of you, but you're on my list." He taps his tiny notepad. "It's suspicious that you happened to find the body out here when it's clear the murder didn't happen this morning."

Agnes frowns, wagging her finger at the sheriff. "You ought to know better than to jump to conclusions like that. We wouldn't have called you if we were guilty."

Sheriff Flowers points to me. "You didn't call me. The new girl did."

He knows my name. We've met several times before. I wonder at what point people will start calling me Charlotte McKay and stop referring to me as the new girl.

"Of course Charlotte called. She's the only one with a phone on her."

I guess that's a city behavior I haven't outgrown yet. It would never occur to me back when I was living in Chicago to go anywhere without my cell phone. Life moves slower in Sweetwater Falls. There isn't as much cause for panic, or fear of being stranded somewhere. The population is small, and so is the town. It would be perfect here...

...if not for the murder.

Logan's shoulders lower. "You called the station? You have my phone number," he reminds me, looking slightly betrayed.

My cheeks heat so hot and so quickly, I'm fairly certain I might burst into flames. "I called the... Isn't it right I should call the police?" I touch my forehead, no doubt smearing more manure on my face.

Logan holds up his hands. "Yes, of course." He lowers his voice. "I only meant that you can call me, too. I haven't heard from you in a few weeks."

That's because when we went to the lemonade festival, I choked on a cup of lemonade and sprayed some of the acidic liquid out my nose when he looked into my eyes for too long.

There's no coming back from that sort of embarrassment. I should think Logan would be glad to get some space from me and my ridiculous crush. "I'mma get to the... So you can do the murder thing."

Sheriff Flowers doesn't have a good reason to keep us around, only his suspicions. He lets us go so he can deal with the body, and I can continue hiding from Logan Flowers.

3

RUMORS

*W*aitressing is not my calling, to put it mildly. Waiting tables at an outdated diner that doesn't serve homemade desserts is a hit to my pride. I love the smell of freshly baked cupcakes and buttercream so thick it could very well be spread on toast.

As I slide a plate of the diner's generic cherry pie to the person sitting in the booth, I fight the urge to apologize to them for the poor quality. Bill, the owner of the diner and my boss, has no interest in upgrading from frozen desserts to fresh ones. So I serve desserts I would never eat myself to people who pay money for them.

Yuck. The crust looks anemic.

There isn't a single bakery in Sweetwater Falls for me to beg for a chance to work in their kitchen. But that doesn't stop me from baking. It's my outlet, my breath of fresh air when I get bogged down with too many worries crowding my thoughts.

It's usually not this crowded in Bill's Diner, but it didn't take long for word to spread that I was the one who stumbled over the dead body.

Bill isn't a particularly cheery person in general, but when his diner is full, he is Father Christmas. He comes out of the kitchen, wiping his greasy hands off on his apron. He grins at the family who just walked in, his bushy eyebrows raised. "Welcome! Glad to have you here. Have you tried our soup of the day?"

It's broccoli cheese soup. It's always broccoli cheese soup. I used to like broccoli cheese soup before I started working here. The cheese broth is sort of rubbery with a burnt aftertaste.

But business is steady today, so I can't complain.

Or I can't complain out loud, I guess.

The teenaged hostess pops her pink gum. "Right this way."

When she moves toward my section, I shake my head. "My shift is up. You might want to seat them in Judy's section."

Bill's thick brows push together as he swipes at his bulbous nose. "You can't clock out yet. It's a zoo in here!"

I fix Bill with unconcealed displeasure. "I've been here all morning."

"One more hour?" He presses his greasy hands together. "We're getting backed up in the kitchen!" He says it with such happiness that I can't turn him down. Besides, Bill is rarely jolly. Might as well reward the good behavior when it happens.

By the time the hour passes, I've given my standard, "Yes, I found the dead body in the field," reply no less than five dozen times since my shift started. I can imagine the scandalous gossip is the only reason people would suffer through what Bill calls a shepherd's pie (which contains no lamb and bears no resemblance to its namesake. It's comprised of dry mashed potatoes with chunky beef gravy, and like, four peas). The tables are still full and there's a line out the door, even though I have nothing of interest to add to what everyone apparently already knows.

Word has spread far and wide that I tripped over a dead body in the field. People all know that the body has yet to be identified, but it's widely speculated to be the personal trainer and young lover of Lisa Swanson.

The only thing I could possibly add was that the man appeared to have been strangled to death, but that's not a detail I want to talk about. Just picturing the gruesome bruises around his neck is a horror I'm still not over.

Bill begs again for me to stay, but I need to wash the French fry stink out of my hair before it becomes permanent.

Also, I have a feeling that he would ask me to work all day and all night, so I know I have to cut him off at some point.

Plus, I haven't seen Marianne in two whole days, which is a world record for us. Usually either she stops by the diner on her way into the library, or I stop by the library after my shift, so we can sit together and chat about all we missed in each other's lives in the few hours since we talked last. But being that the library has been closed this week for renovations to the roof, we haven't been able to get together.

I trot to my red sedan and plop my black waitressing apron in the passenger's seat, grateful to be rid of it. But before I can turn the key in the ignition, a knock sounds at my door.

I startle in my seat before rolling down my window. "Can I help you?" I ask with a tired smile.

The woman has dyed blond hair and black eyebrows. She looks to be in her fifties and is wearing a sun hat with a long brim to shield her face. "You're the new girl, right? Winifred's niece?"

I take my keys out of the ignition and open up the door, standing beside her in the parking lot. "I am, but I'm not interested in talking about the incident in the field. Whoever that man is has a right to his privacy, so I'm just going to let the police handle the whodunnits of the whole thing."

The woman exhales as if I've just told her she can have a million dollars. "I'm glad to hear you say that. You're absolutely right. His death should be a tragedy, not fodder for conjecture and town gossip. He was a sweet guy." The woman tears up, so I scramble to offer her a napkin from my waitressing apron.

"Oh, hun. I'm so sorry. Did you know him?"

The woman nods, blowing her nose into the brittle one-ply napkin. "I did. So awful. I saw the pictures yesterday. I thought I was okay to leave the house, but maybe it's too soon. I just wanted to see you. I know you found the body, but I wanted to make sure you weren't spreading around town anything bad about how you found him."

I blanche at the notion. "Of course not. It's not my business." Her words ping in my brain. "You saw pictures. Did you speak with the sheriff?"

She casts around skittishly, making sure her face stays hidden from passersby in the parking lot. "He showed me how... I still can't believe Jared is gone!"

Ah. Jared. Much better than "Young Stallion".

My hand finds its way to her back, rubbing soothing circles into her spine. She's a slender woman but not skinny. She has toned biceps that her tank top clearly displays. Though I'm still taller than she is, it's only by an inch or so.

"You poor thing. I didn't realize he had friends in Sweetwater Falls. I'm so sorry. Were you close?"

The woman scoffs, though I'm not sure why. "You can probably guess we were. The whole town has an opinion on that. I'm sure it's all anyone's been talking about."

Realization dawns on me, but I need it confirmed. "We haven't met yet. I'm Charlotte McKay." This woman doesn't have a friend in this town right now, I'm guessing. While I don't condone cheating of any kind, I also don't condone listening to rumors and making up my mind about a person before I've met them.

At least, I try not to be that person.

The woman blinks at me, and I can tell by her confusion that she's reevaluating our entire exchange. "You really are new in town. You're being nice to me."

"Should I be mean? You've clearly just lost a friend."

Lisa breaks down all over again. "I'm Lisa. Lisa Swanson. Everyone thinks I had an affair with Jared, but Wesley and I know the truth. Wesley is my husband. Now Jared's turned up dead and it's bringing up all of this..." She motions to her wet eyes, hiccupping through her sadness. "I just wanted to talk to you to make sure you weren't embarrassing Jared's memory. He didn't deserve..." She tears up all over again.

I shake my head, still rubbing my palm across her back. "No, no. All I've told people is the truth: that I was in the field on cleanup duty the morning after the fair. I tripped over a body. Until you told me his name, I didn't know it."

She blows her nose into the napkin again. "Those rumors are all anyone thinks about when my name comes up in conversation. I don't know why Jared was even in Sweetwater Falls! He lives two towns over."

My mouth pulls to the side. "That is odd. I wonder why he was here. Maybe he loves petting zoos." It's a poor offering of a reason, but it's my best guess.

Lisa releases a gentle scoff. "Jared's allergic to peanuts, hay and most things outdoors." She blinks rapidly because her mascara is starting to run, gumming her eyelashes together. "You don't think he was coming here to see me, do you?"

I grimace, uncertain how I landed myself in this conversation. "I mean, you would know better than I would." I don't want to cut our conversation short, but there are people pressing their noses to the diner's long picture window. "Look, I was going to head home and make some cupcakes. Do you want to come? You sound like you've had a rough couple of days. Talking things out might be a good place to start."

Lisa angles her chin toward me, her lower lip quivering. "That is the nicest thing. Thank you. Everyone knows that my 'secret lover' was just murdered, but not a single person has reached out. I'm not sure what I was expecting. I've been the town joke for years."

"Well, lucky for you, I'm new here, so I'm only interested in cupcakes and making new friends. You sound like you could use both of those things."

Lisa exhales and throws her arms around my neck. "Thank you. This has been the worst few days of my life. Are you sure? Having me in your home won't exactly win you any popularity points."

I clutch my pretend pearls. "Oh, no!"

Lisa chuckles, despite her tears, and steps back from my car. "You're living at Winifred's house, right?"

"Sure am. See you in a few."

I watch her walk to her car to make sure no one bothers her before I start my engine and back out of my parking space.

Apparently her affair was only a rumor, but her pal is still dead. She might need a new friend.

Especially now that Jared has turned up dead with the killer still on the loose.

4

LISA'S INVESTMENT

*T*he white colonial with pale blue shutters is empty when I get there. Aunt Winifred mentioned she was going to be out with the girls, planning their next activity.

I ask very few questions because whatever the Live Forever Club gets up to, I usually don't want to know. Plausible deniability. Also, if I know about their plans, they often invite me along. I'm in no mood for skinny dipping or skydiving, so I was more than happy to kiss my great aunt goodbye this morning before I left for work.

I hold the door open for Lisa and welcome her inside. The front room is entirely Winifred, decked in doilies with antique furniture and mauve curtains hanging from ornate curtain rods.

The kitchen is far cheerier. "Come on in. Let me fix you a cup of tea." I escort Lisa into my favorite room of the house, smiling at the happy yellow walls and brightly painted cupboards. "How long have you lived in Sweetwater Falls?" I ask her.

"Oh, all my life. That's everyone's story, pretty much. My family's been here for generations. No place better to live on

God's green earth, unless you find yourself in the center of a scandal."

I don't know what to say to that. I shouldn't pry. The woman is fragile and dealing with a lot. But she brought up the subject, so I lean in. "Tell me about Jared."

She sits at the round table in the dining area of the kitchen. Her fingernails drum on the surface while she stares at nothing, her eyes unfocused. "To tell you about Jared, I'd have to tell you about Wesley."

I pull down a tin of the chamomile Winnie always makes me when I'm too worked up. "Then tell me about Wesley."

A tender expression sweeps across her face. "We've been married for thirty years. High school sweethearts. We were so young back then. Babies. Thought things would always be simple. But it never is." She casts around for something to dab at her eyes, so I trot into the bathroom and fetch the box of tissues and set it on the table for her. "Thank you."

"No problem." I fill the kettle and start it heating on the stovetop, but my hands still itch to do something I enjoy while I listen to Lisa's story.

My palms always itch when I need to bake. It's not a want; it's a desire that starts deep down in my soul and nags at me until I'm elbow deep in flour and frosting.

So I tug down the container of sugar, along with baking soda, salt and various other ingredients without a true plan in my head as to how they're going to come together.

That's never my main concern; the cupcakes ingredients always find a way to sing. In fact, I happen to think they turn out better when I don't have a plan.

"Wesley and I have a good life together, but roofing isn't always steady work." She blows her nose into the tissue. "He would have seasons where he would sit on the couch for weeks at a time, and then others where he was working insane hours. I would go for days without seeing him. When business is good, it's great, but when it's bad, it's horrible."

"That makes sense." Even though Lisa already told me she didn't step out on her marriage, I brace myself for the lonely hearts tale of a woman justifying an affair to me.

These are not my favorite types of conversations.

"Wesley's business was doing well for the moment, which is great, but that meant I was alone." She plucks another tissue from the box. "So I joined a gym in Hamshire. Got myself a personal trainer. Started looking for opportunities that might help even things out."

I bite down on my lip, keeping my back to her so the condemnation doesn't radiate out from me. I didn't invite Lisa over to judge her. I invited her over because she's grieving and she's alone. I dump a fair drizzle of oil into the bowl, thinking that if I was grieving and washing myself in guilt every day, I would want nothing short of double fudge everything. Next comes some sugar, then a bit of yogurt to give the chocolate flavor a little lift to it with a tang at the end of each bite. I hum to myself as I set the mixer whirling.

Lisa sets her hat atop the table, exposing her messy bun to me because hopefully she knows she is in a safe place here. "I got to talking with Jared—my personal trainer—and learned we had similar interests. His dream was to open an exclusive, upscale gym."

My head tilts to the side. This is not what I was expecting her to say. "He didn't like being a personal trainer?"

"No, no. He loved it. But like everyone, he had dreams of doing more. Being his own boss."

"O-kay," I reply, drawing out the word because we're getting further and further away from the affair I'm certain she is going to come clean about.

"I love to exercise, and I have a business degree." She

motions with her hand palm-upward, lowering her chin. "Granted, a rather dusty degree I haven't used in years, but still. I sat down with him once a week and we started to build his business together. It was exciting to be part of something, to build instead of feeling helpless. I wanted in. The plan was solid, and so was his work, so I invested a small amount to get him started."

My words come out slow. "How much is a small amount?"

Lisa turns her head from me. "Ten thousand dollars. Wesley's job was going well. I asked him if we could invest it, and he was okay with the amount."

"Alright. That sounds like a nice venture. Did it get off the ground?"

"No." Her voice catches as her volume climbs. "Not too long ago, Jared and I were about to pull the trigger on his business, but he needed a little more capital. So he came to the house to speak with Wesley, asking him for a loan." She shook her head. "That conversation did not go well. Wesley was mad that after ten grand, Jared still hadn't done a day of work. Jared was frustrated because it takes more than that to start a business if you want to really get anywhere, and we were his only investors. They argued a bit, but that was that. Then Jared left." She lowers her chin. "That's when the rumors really started."

"Rumors?" I add a dash of vanilla to the mix and crack two eggs into the bowl while the beaters work their magic.

Lisa wheels her hand in the air while she talks. "That I was having an affair with my personal trainer, and Wesley caught us in the act. Of course, no such thing ever happened, but you know how people can be when they're presented with fresh gossip."

I gape at her, turning off the mixer. "Are you telling me that you never had an affair with Jared?"

Lisa's face pulls. "Please. He's young enough to be my child. No, of course not. I love Wesley and I've never cheated."

"You do realize everyone in Sweetwater Falls is convinced you were having an affair for like, a long time, right?"

Lisa shrugs. "'Small minds, small talk,' my mother used to say. It never bothered me all that much. I should have set the rumors straight a long time ago, but no one listened. Then when people overheard Wesley and Jared arguing, I never had a chance of stopping that from spreading through the town like wildfire."

"Oh, Lisa. I'm so sorry. And now your friend is dead. You really didn't know he was at the Farmer's Fair?"

Lisa shakes her head. "He's allergic to hay. I can't imagine he would go there. And he and Wesley hadn't exactly left things on the greatest note, so I don't know why he would come here. Maybe to make amends?"

I nod. "It's possible." Then I straighten. "No, it's more than possible. I'm going to believe that's why Jared came into town. He wanted to make sure he had a good relationship with his friends and investors. Let's believe the best."

Lisa nods, swiping at the mascara running down her cheek. "But then the question is still there: who killed Jared?"

I have no answers for her, so I close my mouth while my mind starts working overtime.

While I have no idea who could have done this to the young entrepreneur, I do know that he most likely didn't deserve to die and be left in a field.

5

MOCHA LATTE AND CUPCAKES

Two days after discovering that Lisa Swanson's salacious secret wasn't an affair, but rather a business investment gone wrong, I am no closer to figuring out who might be behind Jared's untimely death.

Though not for lack of trying.

I'm supposed to meet Lisa for coffee at The Snuggle Inn after my shift so we can talk a bit more about how she's processing all of this. Even though I'm new to Sweetwater Falls, I wonder if I am Lisa's only female friend. I really hope I'm wrong on that.

Just in case, I asked Lisa if I could bring Marianne along, to which she happily agreed. Though we are half her age, Lisa is grateful for the companionship. In case they don't hit it off, I brought double fudge cupcakes—the ones I started making while Lisa was pouring her heart out to me in the kitchen. I figure there isn't much that double fudge can't fix.

Marianne, however, is dubious. "I still don't believe she wasn't having an affair. I mean, the rumors have been going around for a long time that she's been stepping out on Wesley with her personal trainer."

"I'm telling you, that's not what happened. They were going into business together, and that's that."

Marianne sips her coffee with a narrowed eye. "Hmm."

"Oh, give her a chance. She just lost her friend."

Marianne sets her mug down. "Oh, okay. You really believe her?"

"I have no reason not to."

Marianne sits back in her seat, crossing her arms over her chest. "She could be the killer, you know. You might have been alone in the house with the Young Stallion's killer."

I snort into my mocha latte. "His name is Jared."

"I'm sure it is." Marianne raises her nose in the air, begging me to tweak it for her impertinence. Though I can't exactly blame her. I bought into the same rumor until I heard the truth straight from Lisa's mouth.

When the door to the kitchen swings open, none other than Fisher comes out. His black curls are stuck to his forehead with sweat, his round face smiling at me. "If it isn't the only girl who needs her coffee cut with hot chocolate."

I raise my cup to him. "I prefer to pretend it's a mocha latte, made just for me."

"It is made just for you. No one else would ruin a good cup of coffee like that."

I stand to give him a big hug. "You've been working nonstop all week. I haven't played video games with you in far too long."

Fisher squeezes me around the ribs with his giant forearms. He's burly, with a small hint of a belly puffing over the apron wound about his waist. Though Fisher is in his forties, he plays video games like a teenager. It's where I get all my best trash talk out.

"You're addicted to gaming," Fisher chides me, though nothing could be further from the truth. It's him I look forward to seeing, not the stupid avatars. "I've been putting in massive overtime, trying to get us back up and running."

"I figured you might need some extra energy." I lift the lid of the pink box I brought along with me and pull out a double fudge cupcake.

Fisher's face lights up. The two of us understand that the best gift one kitchen rat can give another is something home-made. "I was hoping you were baking again. When I take a break, this is what I'm having."

Though the owner of the Snuggle Inn stepped down, Fisher informed me that the nightshift manager is filling those shoes now, however wobbly. "You've been so busy lately. How's Lenny handling the added responsibilities?" I ask him, leaning in so as not to make the other diners question that perhaps they are not in the most experienced of hands.

Fisher shrugs. "Paychecks have been promised to come on time, so I can't complain. I didn't know you'd be stopping by today. To what do I owe the pleasure?"

"I wanted the best mocha latte Sweetwater Falls has to offer, plus a plate of whatever you're most excited about that's on the menu."

Fisher slaps his hands together. "Coming right up. And that's the only semi-mocha anything Sweetwater Falls will ever have to offer. People around here like their coffee to taste like coffee."

I toss my blonde curls over my shoulder. "The heathens."

Fisher turns to Marianne and slaps her hand. "How about you, Miss Head Librarian? I'm almost finished with the book on the history of eggs that you sent over."

Marianne beams at him, angling her shoulders forward. "Oh, isn't it fascinating? How the grading system of egg density and the air pockets came into play had me turning pages for hours."

Only Marianne.

She slides the unopened menu towards him. "I'll have what she's having."

When Lisa approaches our table with clear timidity on her features, Fisher straightens. "Hello, Fisher. Could I get a cup of coffee?"

"You're joining Charlotte and Marianne?"

She nods and takes a seat at our table. "Thank you."

Fisher shoots me a look that tells me he will eventually demand the whole story of why I am dining with Lisa Swanson, then he shuffles off toward the kitchen.

"Hi, girls. Good to see you, Marianne. Charlotte suggested I get out more, so I don't sit around the house all depressed by myself." She spreads out her arms to us. "Now I get to bring down the both of you with my glum mood! Lucky you."

Despite her belief that Lisa is no good, Marianne chuckles at the faux cheer in her tone. "I'm properly caffeinated, so don't hold back." She raises her coffee mug to toast the sadness.

There are a few bumpy starts, but Marianne is a good listener while Lisa opens up. By the time the food arrives, Lisa has truly let down her guard, and Marianne has started to let her naturally compassionate side shine.

"You lost your friend. It's normal to be angry, sad, depressed, confused. All of those things make complete sense."

Lisa hangs her head. "Is it wrong of me to secretly feel cheated? All that money we invested is gone now." She scrunches her nose and shakes her head at herself. "That's not the thing to focus on. I know that. But my mind keeps bouncing back to it. Thousands of dollars, gone."

Marianne extends her hand to rest it on Lisa's wrist. "You're going through a lot. I'm sure you'll have even more unexpected feelings that pop up before the dust settles."

Lisa's shoulders slump. "Thank you for saying that. I know

it's a horrible thing to think at a time like this." Her arms move in a circle in front of her face. "Now that I'm finally talking about everything with women who care, it's all coming out. None of this is pretty."

"It's not supposed to be," I remind her. "Grief is hard, and it takes a long time. But we're here."

It feels good to listen to Lisa, like I'm making a new friendship that goes beyond the level of an acquaintance. I dig into the meal that Fisher made for us. He is an absolute master at making fresh pasta. The handmade mushroom ravioli in a fresh cream and sage sauce is like nothing I've ever tasted before. Each bite is a masterpiece. I feel bad eating so much in front of Lisa, who is sipping on her coffee. She informed us that she hasn't had much of an appetite as of late.

Lisa lowers her head, holding her mug with both hands. "I can't even be properly sad. I'm upset about the lost money. I'm anxious about going back to the gym, which I normally love doing, but now don't feel like I can because Jared isn't there anymore. And then there's the whole thing with the sheriff."

My ears perk up, inching me away from the best lunch I've had in ages. "What about the sheriff?"

Lisa stares into her coffee as if she's hoping it might answer for her so she doesn't have to. "He thinks I had something to do with Jared's death. I didn't. I was at home with Wesley the night it happened. We went to the fair early, but then left after half an hour or so and went home. Still, I guess having your spouse as your alibi is fishy for some reason."

Marianne forks her final bite of ravioli, swiping it through the remains of the sauce. "The police will rule you out as a suspect because you're innocent. Once they do that, they can focus on who else might be involved."

Lisa keeps her eyes on her beverage. "I wish I knew why Jared was at the fair. Did he need something? Was he going to ask for help with the launch of the business?" She lowers her head. "Was he going to ask for more money?" Then she shakes her head. "It doesn't matter. None of that matters anymore. I can't believe he's gone."

I don't have the right words to offer, but I do have cupcakes. Since we're finished with our meal, and Fisher doesn't mind if I bring in my own dessert (so long as I bring him some), I pop open the lid of the pink box. "I think grief is paired best with double fudge."

Lisa laughs airily through her nose. "I think you're right about that. Where did you get these? I know they're not from any restaurant in Sweetwater Falls."

Marianne jumps in, eagerly advertising my talents for me, because that's what good friends do. "She bakes them herself. Invents her own recipes."

Lisa takes one of the desserts and peels back the wrapper. "I suppose if I'm not going to the gym, I might as well give myself something to work off when I do go back."

My favorite part about baking for other people is watching them take their first bite. The inhale, the exhale and the "mm" noise invigorates my soul and validates my passion. If I could bake all day and watch people enjoy my creations, I could die a happy woman. I can't imagine life getting better than that.

Lisa does not disappoint. "Mm! Oh, honey. These aren't cupcakes. These are therapy. What did you put in this?"

My grin lights up my whole demeanor. "Chocolate with a side of chocolate."

"Maybe it's just been so long since I've had a proper dessert that didn't have the words 'sugar-free' or 'low-fat' on them, but this is heavenly."

Now I'm beaming.

"Tell me Bill is going to put these on his menu. I would imagine that's the only thing people would order."

"Nah. Bill doesn't like change. I was selling them here for a bit, but now that The Snuggle Inn is under new ownership, they're not at a place where they can contract out desserts anymore."

Lisa swipes her finger through the frosting while Marianne's eyes roll back as she munches on her cupcake. "Can I order some? Do you do that? My in-laws are coming in from out of town next week. I would love to serve them something that would blow their minds." She casts me a look of frustration. "The big family joke is that I can't cook. Hilarious."

Marianne hops in. "She sure does. Charlotte bakes from her kitchen and sells them as needed. It's a new business, but she wants to eventually do this full-time. Minimum order is a dozen." Marianne is no stranger to putting her foot down and being bold if it's someone else she is standing up for. She rattles off a price that makes me grimace. It's three times what it costs me to bake them. I know that's standard good business practice: one-third to cover the cost of the ingredients, one-third to pay yourself, and one-third to pay for the building. But seeing as I'm baking out of the kitchen at home, I hardly think I need to charge the extra third.

Marianne's mouth firms as she moves her foot under the table. She steps on my toe to keep me from negotiating myself out of a paycheck.

Lisa bats her hand. "They're easily worth more than that. You take tips, right?"

"What?"

Lisa leans forward. "Is this a hobby, or is this a passion?"

Before I can stop myself, I'm answering honestly. "It's my passion. I love baking cupcakes. It makes me come alive. If the world was filled with cupcakes, I'm not sure there's a problem that couldn't be solved."

I didn't realize I had all that poetry in me. Even Marianne's mouth drops.

Lisa smiles with no hint of derision. "Then put me on the list as your loyal customer. My in-laws are coming over next week, but I think I'll want to set up a monthly order."

I gape at her. "Are you serious?" It's the wrong thing to ask, but it can't possibly be this easy to get clients.

"This month, I would love this double fudge kind, but next month, surprise me." She pulls out a crinkly receipt from her purse and a pen, laying the paper flat on the table. "I think it's time I stopped hiding from my neighbors. Do you have business cards?"

"Wait, this is all happening too fast. Business cards?"

Lisa pauses and meets my eyes. "Do you want your dreams to come true now, or in forty years?"

Her question levels my excuses and silences the fear that I won't be a good businesswoman. I don't know if I'm the sort of person who has talent enough to take my passion seriously, but Lisa's determined stare tells me now is the time to try.

I swallow hard. "Now. Not in forty years. I want to be a baker and control my own flavors now. I want to make people smile and mute their grief with a cupcake. I want to spread sugar and sweetness."

More poetry. I only get like this when I talk about cupcakes.

"That's your passion, and this is mine." Lisa taps her pen to the back of the receipt. "I have a business degree that's been collecting dust. I love making business plans. I love marketing. *My* dream is to help other people achieve *their* dreams." Emotion sweeps across her face. "That's what I was doing for Jared. Please, let me be pushy. Let me help you get this off the ground. I need a project, or I'll go crazy with grief."

I cast a look of sheer trepidation at Marianne, who looks on the verge of squealing with giddy delight. I open my mouth to agree to take the help and her reoccurring order, but Marianne beats me to it, bursting with glee. "Yes! Thank you. We've been trying to work with a restaurant or a place like this that has a commercial kitchen and clientele, but it keeps falling through. Baking out of her home and filling orders that way is perfect!"

I bite down on my lower lip. "Do you really think I can drum up clients?"

Lisa snorts with a smile on her face as she jots notes down on the back of the receipt. "I think that part is already taken care of. I'm making a short list of supplies you'll need to get this thing off the ground. Do you have a business license?"

My eyes widen. "Business license? No. I just bake for friends."

Lisa's gaze connects with mine. "And I build business plans for friends." She finishes jotting down a few more things and then passes the receipt to me. "Here's a short list, but these things take time and effort. One thing at a time, starting with applying for a business license. The website is written down for you, but you'll need the thing notarized."

Marianne nearly shouts, "I know a notary!"

The urge to tell them both that I am not worth all this fuss is overwhelming, but before I can work out a protest, Marianne shoves her finger in my face. With almost everyone else, she is meek as a lamb, but the upside to being best friends is that we don't have to hold back with each other. "I know you're freaking out, but before you tell her to stop because you're not ready or not worth it, let me tell you that you *are* worth it. And if you're not ready, you have me. You have Aunt Winnie and the Live Forever Club."

Lisa puts her pen back into her purse. "And you have me."

My eyes dot with moisture. I feel so unworthy of such love and attention. "I really wasn't trying to milk you for free business advice by making you a cupcake. I wanted to do something nice for you."

Lisa smirks at me. "I know. And this is me, doing something nice for you. And frankly, something selfish for me. I need a distraction from this whole Jared mess." Then she lets out a grunt of frustration and rubs her forehead. "And I just remembered I have to pick up the yoga mat I ordered, so I have to go back to the gym. I've been avoiding the place."

"Understandable," Marianne supplies.

Curiosity tugs at the back of my brain. Before I can really think it through, I speak up. "I could pick up the yoga mat for you."

Lisa sits up. "You don't have to do that. We barely know each other. I'm just being a baby about it all."

"No, you're grieving. There's a big difference. And you shouldn't have to tackle anything you don't absolutely need to right now."

Marianne nods. "I'll go with you. The sooner you get your yoga mat, the better. Isn't it supposed to be stress relieving?"

Lisa blinks at Marianne. "You've never done yoga before?"

Marianne's neck shrinks as she fiddles with her braid. "No. It looks like it's for people who know what they're doing in a gym. I'm not all that bendy."

Lisa softens. "Oh, that's not true at all. Yoga is perfect for anyone who wants a lot of serenity and a little extra flexibility. How about this: if you two go pick up my yoga mat for me, I'll do a little yoga session for you. I swear, it's lifechanging."

Marianne's timidity is evenly paired with her desire to be truly wild and try things outside of her limited comfort zone. "That might be nice."

I agree for the both of us before Marianne can talk herself out of trying something new. "It's a deal."

Lisa scribbles down the address of the gym, but over her

shoulder I see two people whispering behind their hands while staring at our table. From their narrowed eyes and pointed glares, I can tell they disapprove of Lisa having friends.

No matter that I can see she is clearly innocent; it seems much of the town has already made up its mind.

Lisa Swanson will be guilty in their eyes unless we can prove she didn't commit murder.

6

RECEIPT

*M*arianne is a good friend. Perhaps she's vying for friend of the year or something, because on the way to the gym after we finish up our lunch with Lisa, Marianne copies down the list of things I'll need to do to make my home business official, so we both have a copy of the list.

My hands grip the steering wheel while I keep my eyes on the road. "This is much, right? Like, did I just accidentally take advantage of a grieving woman? I didn't mean for her to feel like she had to make me a business plan. It didn't even occur to me to start a business out of the home. Is that even legal?"

Marianne scours the back of the receipt where Lisa wrote down my to-do list to get me started. "It looks like you'll need a business license, which is no big deal. And yes, this is perfectly legal. Lisa mentioned the Cottage Food law, which is the provision that allows people to do what you're going to be doing— selling food you've prepared in your home."

"This is crazy! Business license? I'm just me. I'm not a business."

Marianne is unconcerned with my fretting. "The first thing we need to do is clear it with Winifred to make sure she's cool with it." Marianne tugs her phone out of her purse and connects the call before I can wrap my mind around how to ask for such a thing. I mean, I was baking in the kitchen in the house when I was selling my cupcakes for other businesses, but this feels different.

Marianne is chipper as ever. "Hey, Winnie. Charlotte was thinking of opening up a baking business to fill orders from individuals, rather than restaurants. Might mean more cupcakes get made in your kitchen. That cool with you?"

Great Aunt Winifred's response needs no clarification. "Yes! Do it today! Start now! Do I need to hit the Colonel's General Store for ingredients?"

Marianne giggles. "No. That's all we needed. Just the green light from you. Now it has its proper blessing."

"Tell my honey cake that I love her, and I want to be her first customer."

"Actually, she already has a customer!"

"Darn it all! I wanted to be first. Oh, fine. Second, at least. And I want Agnes to look at that pricing sheet to make sure Charlotte's not underbidding herself."

"On it!"

"Tell my girl that I'm so proud of her. Charlotte the Brave!"

My heart tugs because I didn't realize how badly I do want Aunt Winnie's approval—a thing she's made clear from the beginning I've always had. Each time I hear it, my heart feels bolder.

When Marianne turns to me after ending the call, we are both breathless. "First thing on the list, done. Second, we need to think of a name for the business. Well, that's easy. Next is we..."

"Whoa, what? Since when do we have a name?" I reach over the console to squeeze her hand. "And by the way, I love that you keep saying 'we'. There's no way I would even try this without my lovely assistant."

Marianne bats her lashes at me and flips her braid over her shoulder. "The loveliest. And of course we're doing this together. One of us has to be the mean one—setting respectable prices and making sure you get paid."

Neither of us expect me to do more than chortle at Marianne's self-assessment, but I surprise us both with a hearty belly laugh as I turn off the freeway toward our destination. "You're the mean one? Is that your role? I had no idea. Best tell the villagers to scatter when they catch wind that Marianne the Terrible is on the warpath."

Marianne sticks to her guns. "You just watch. No one messes with my bestest."

Sweetness coats the inside of my red sedan. My smile matches hers. "You're my bestest, too."

"Then it's settled. I'm the mean one, and we already have a name for the business."

"What's the name?"

Charlotte blinks at me, as if the answer should be obvious. "The Bravery Bakery, specializing in the world's best honey cakes."

The hairs on my arms stand up as if the name hitting the air has shot me with a dose of electricity and possibility. This is what people must feel when they confront their destiny head on.

"I love it," I whisper. "It's perfect."

"This is a good idea." She holds up the receipt. "I'm glad we met with Lisa."

"I'm glad I have you."

I love our friendship so much that I don't let go of her hand until I absolutely have to if I want to park the car in the narrow spots of the gym's parking lot.

It takes me some finagling to park neatly between the yellow lines, but after I manage it, I heave a gust of relief and turn to Marianne, expecting a high five.

Worry washes over her face as she stares at the scrap of paper in her hand.

"What? Marianne, what's wrong?"

"Lisa told us that she went to the fair with Wesley when it started, and she stayed for half an hour or so, right?"

"Yeah. Then they went home for the night. The sheriff isn't happy with her story," I recall from our luncheon, "because having your spouse as your alibi is a gray area or something."

"Why do you think that is?" Marianne purses her lips, her eyes focused on the receipt. Only now I can see that she's not staring at the scribbled to-do list; she's looking at the black ink printed on the receipt from whatever store Lisa went to recently.

I shrug. "I dunno. Probably because a spouse might tell a lie to protect the love of their life. Doesn't mean Lisa's guilty, though. Just because Wesley is her alibi doesn't mean she doesn't have one." My frown begins to match Marianne's when she hands the slip of paper to me.

"Look at this, Charlotte."

My brows bunch together as I squint at the information typed at the top. "From the day Jared was murdered. This store isn't in Sweetwater Falls. A pack of gum and eight ounces of peanut oil." I blink at the paper, my chest tightening. "Oh, no."

"That receipt is timestamped, Charlotte," Marianne points out.

That's not the part I was focused on, but it's no small concern. "Lisa was shopping after going to the Farmer's Fair, instead of going straight home, like she said she did. But that's not the worst of it, Marianne."

"It's not? Because it seems pretty bad from where I sit."

My tongue slides across my lower lip. "Name me one thing you might buy peanut oil for."

Marianne's mouth pulls to the side. "I'm not sure. Maybe stir fry?"

"Miss no sugar and no fat is buying peanut oil to make stir fry? I don't think so."

Marianne takes the receipt back to look it over again. "Then what? I'm missing the big scandal. What's so upsetting about her buying gum and peanut oil?"

I close my eyes as a clue I don't want to look at slides into place. "When Lisa came over, she mentioned that Jared was allergic to all sorts of things—mainly hay and peanuts."

Marianne's mouth falls open. "What? No. You don't think Lisa bought peanut oil and poisoned Jared, do you? She was brokenhearted over his death."

My own buried doubts begin to surface. "She kept mentioning how much money she lost, investing in his business." Then I shake my head. "But where's the logic in killing someone you've already invested money in? She wanted him to succeed, not for him to die."

Marianne folds the receipt carefully, now that it might be evidence. "I don't know what it means. Maybe nothing. Or..."

I lean forward, resting my forehead on the steering wheel. "Or maybe Lisa murdered Jared because she knew he'd swindled her out of ten thousand dollars."

My shoulders slump, wishing life could be simple, and that dreams of cupcakes could come without scandal.

7

JARED MEMORABILIA

The gym is crowded. For me that would make this a place at which I would never work out. There's a room with an aerobics class of some sort happening, but the leader's microphone is so loud that I have to shout to Marianne to be heard, even though she is right next to me.

Marianne works in a quiet library all day. I can tell by her wide eyes and caged animal body language that she is enduring sheer sensory overwhelm. She clings to my arm—a small town cutie confronted with the bustle of life outside of Sweetwater Falls.

When the front desk clerk asks to see our gym membership cards, I explain the situation. "But I'm not sure where to go to pick up the yoga mat Lisa ordered."

The woman at the front desk is peppy and looks overly caffeinated, her high ponytail bouncing as she bops to the left. "The store is just that way."

Marianne doesn't let go of my arm the entire way to the busy shop. The room is about as big as a convenience store, but it is filled with at least three dozen people, all either looking at products or standing in the long line to buy something. The room is

stacked to the ceiling with shelves of protein powder and nutri-
tional supplements.

Instinctively I suck in my stomach, unable to recall the last
time I went to a gym.

Marianne's face twists in horror. "Is that... Oh my goodness."

I follow her gaze to a poster on the wall of none other than
Jared. I gasp at the scrawl next to what is clearly the picture
taken from his employee ID. The words "Look like me for eternity" are printed next to his head, and beside the giant picture is
a table of supplements and protein bars, all with Jared's picture
stuck onto each bottle and wrapper. "Did they make his face into
a sticker?"

Marianne looks like she might be sick. "They're using his
face to sell stuff."

I migrate through the crowd to the display. Only unlike
everyone else, I'm not there to buy anything with Jared's face on
it. There's a stack of printouts lying on the narrow table, which I
pick up and start reading to Marianne.

"'Jared Harrison was beloved by everyone at Heathren Gym.
He was so much more than a personal trainer, as all of the
employees here are. Jared loved going for runs with the Marathon
Club, and pushed his clients to be at their best, always going the
extra twenty-six-point-two miles. His favorite breakfast was a
Heathren's vanilla protein powder shake, and he was always seen
around the gym snacking on the Heathren's cookie dough
flavored protein bar. His favorite exercises were...'" I balk at the
page. "It's a commercial for their products. This is disgusting."

"Keep it for Lisa. She might want it."

I can't imagine anyone who actually cared about Jared
wanting to read this garbage, but I fold it up and stick it in my
purse.

The line is long, and Marianne looks like she might have a

panic attack from so many people crammed into this small a space. "You go wait out in the hallway," I suggest. "I'll get the yoga mat and we can get out of here."

She doesn't need to be told twice.

The line behind us is out the door when I finally get to the front and request the yoga mat Lisa previously purchased. They check the purchase ID number and disappear into the back to retrieve it.

"I can't believe Jared is dead. I heard they fired him the day before he was found dead, and that's why he killed himself."

The person beside me checking out gasps. "Oh, that's terrible. I don't even know if I want a membership here if that's how bad things get."

Though, as she says this, she is purchasing two tubs of protein powder with Jared's face stuck on the label.

Another person in the line pipes up. "Hello, Jared was hitting up his personal training clients to invest in his own startup. They had every right to fire him." Then his tone softens. "Not that I wish him dead or anything. That's a tragedy. But what were they supposed to do? Let him keep hounding his clients for money?"

At this, I do my best to tune out all other chatter. I thought Lisa was his only investor. I turn to the man, who has a neck about as thick as my waist. "How do you know this? Did Jared ask you to invest?"

The man's head wobbles, which I think counts as a nod. "Sure did. I put in five grand before I had to tell him no more. He was just about to open, too." He waves off his frustration. "Not that money is the thing to think about at a time like this. I'm just saying that the gym can't look the other way if they found out he was trying to start his own gym on the side and using their clients for the startup cash."

"But you still invested, so you must have thought Jared had a good idea. Better than working out here."

The man is wearing a thin tank top and gym shorts and looks like the type who should be a bouncer at a club, though is face isn't entirely unfriendly. "Can you blame me? His plan was dynamite. Exclusive membership. Every membership comes with a personal trainer. The place is limited to fifty people at a time, even during peak gym seasons." He jerks his thumb over his shoulder. "Have you tried to get an elliptical today? And to complete the arms circuit, the line is almost as long as this one. When January hits, I switch my workouts to four in the morning, just so I can get one in. I mean, the facility is nice, don't get me wrong, but to be able to work out in the sort of environment Jared was promising was an offer too good to pass up. Plus, my investment would have guaranteed my membership for five years."

I don't know what to say to all of that.

The person beside me grabs her purchases and leaves, bringing the thick-necked man to stand beside me. I'm a proud five-foot ten inches tall, but this man dwarfs me by about half a foot. "I'm sorry to hear that you lost out on five thousand dollars. Even sorrier that you lost your personal trainer. It sounds like you two spent a lot of time together."

His lips purse as he considers the sympathy that radiates off me. "Thanks. Does it make me a bad person that sometimes I don't know what I'm more upset about losing? A person or five thousand dollars?"

I don't answer his question outright, otherwise I would say, "Obviously." Instead, I opt for gentleness. "I think loss is hard. You're going through a lot right now. Best not judge yourself too harshly until your grief decides how it's going to settle."

Thick-neck turns more fully to me. Were we not mid-conversation, I might judge his body language as confrontational. But his demeanor is softer now as he speaks. "I think that's the wisest thing I've heard in this whole mess. I'm all turned around." He motions to his purchases. "I don't even know why I'm buying this stuff. Guilt, maybe, for feeling sore about the money instead of sore a person just died."

While the woman is scanning his purchases, I take a chance and settle my hand on his wrist. "Don't buy this stuff. Not unless you actually use it."

He chuckles joylessly at himself. "I have about four canisters in my pantry right now. I don't need more."

I assert myself, even though none of this is any of my business. To the clerk, I say, "Can you void those items? He doesn't want them."

His shoulders slump, as if I've just set him free from an obligation he was dreading. "Thanks. I don't want Jared's face in my pantry. That's creepy." His last words are said a little loud and carry above the din.

I turn to see a splintering off of the line as people grimace at the labels of the items in their hands. Perhaps they are judging that they, too, perhaps don't need a sticker of Jared to keep, like an Elvis statue of a memory that is far too fleeting to cherish. I am sure the items they are putting back now would sit in their pantry until the expiration date long passes. They will feel guilty throwing away the picture, but by then the grief will be a small, faded memory.

Doggone, our lives are short.

The woman comes to the counter with Lisa's yoga mat, so I escort the body builder out of the store and into a sliver a clarity.

Marianne's eyebrow hitches when she sees me next to the muscular man, but she doesn't say anything.

He waves his hand in front of his face. "I don't know why I thought I needed to buy that stuff. I'm all turned around."

I tap his elbow and then point to the glass front doors. "I

think you might want to take a walk. It's nice out. Not quite summer, not quite fall."

He squints toward the sunshine as if he hasn't seen natural light in a long time. "That might be nice."

"The machines in the gym are probably all taken anyway. Go for a walk. Spend some time with your grief before trying to reason with it."

His head hangs as if he's been trying to be strong for far too long. "You're a good person. Thanks." He extends his hand to me. "I'm Ivan."

I shake his hand with my free one. "Charlotte." Though we are sharing a moment of true humanity, I have to pry. "Do you know how many investors Jared had?" I wonder if Ivan knows about Lisa.

Ivan chuckles drily. "I know of at least six. All men like me: at the gym long enough to appreciate a good opportunity to work out unbothered when we see it."

All men. So he didn't know about Lisa, which means there might be even more investors cheated out of their money. "And all of them were in for five thousand dollars?"

"Yep. That's the buy-in. He was going to launch it next month, too. Had a location and everything. He needed a little more capital to furnish the place, and then it was a go for launch."

That would be news to Lisa. Jared told her he didn't have a location yet. "Oh yeah? Where was it?"

He swipes his hand over his face. "Not too far from here. I haven't seen it. No point now, I suppose."

My shoulders slump. So much money gone.

"I'll walk you outside, Ivan. It was nice to meet you. I hope you have a better day tomorrow." I motion for Marianne to join us, and the three of us walk out into the sunshine.

The glittery gold does wonders for Ivan's demeanor. After his first few steps into the fresh air, he looks like he can breathe easier, uncluttered by all the Jared memorabilia inside.

The sun does nothing to lift my spirits, however. Even as I bid Ivan farewell, my mind is mired in the possibility that Jared's business might have been a complete and total scam.

8

SWEATING

*A*fter my shift at the diner, I often stop by the library to kill an hour or two before heading home. There's something calming about going from a busy restaurant straight into a building that radiates splendor and quiet. It used to be an old church, back when churches came standard with cathedral architecture, complete with vaulted ceilings, polished floors and stained-glass windows. Even if it wasn't a library, I would still feel the need to lower my voice in reverence whenever entering this beautiful building.

Marianne lets me sort the books that need to be checked in, because that's my favorite part. I like the happy beep the scanner makes when I swipe each book across the gray pad.

"I hate that we were closed for so long. All those people wanting to check out books couldn't read for two weeks!"

I love her tender soul. "You're open now. Or mostly open, anyways."

The work Wesley Swanson's company had to do on the roof of the library and the interior ceiling is finished, but the biographies section is closed off for the final inspection.

Marianne eyes the giant pile of returned books, which is laid out on the rolling rack. "You really don't have to work while you're here. You didn't come for this. You came to hang out."

"Which I'm doing," I remind her cheerily. "Plus, I like scanning things. It's like a hit of dopamine every time it beeps. Like I did something important, even though I know I just picked up a book and put it in a different pile." I motion to the books that need to be shelved again. "You've got the hard part, putting everything back on the shelves in the correct sections."

"I feel guilty that you're doing half my job."

"Unless I'm doing it wrong, you can't stop me." I stick out my tongue at her, to which, she snickers. "Agnes came into the diner today. Asked me if I'd filled out the paperwork for the business license."

Marianne sorts the books into piles, smirking at the mention of her unofficial big sister from the Live Forever Club. "Gotta love them. They're only pushy when it will benefit you." She jerks her head up. "We turned it in, though, right? I'm not imagining that?"

I scan a book with a title that makes me smile. "Quilt Your Troubles Away" sounds like just the sort of book I could use right about now. "Yes, we did. We ordered the business cards and stickers with the logo Aunt Winnie designed to go on my delivery boxes. We have everything we need, including the supplies to complete our very first order, which I'll be doing tomorrow."

I pause to flip open the quilting book. I've never quilted before. The only things I've ever sewn were the pink curtains that used to hang in my childhood bedroom. Still, the promise of doing anything while your troubles melt away sounds incredible.

Marianne continues to sort the books. "You're right. I think worrying is engrained in my DNA. I want this so bad for you." She stands up straighter. "You need a second phone line, or some way people can contact you for orders without blowing up your phone. How's the website coming?"

I groan. "Slow and ugly, but it's finished. I don't know what I'm doing, but I'm learning. My saving grace is that I doubt anyone will ever use it."

"I'm sure it turned out great. And remember, the website is a backup. Most people in Sweetwater Falls don't bother with the internet when they can just show up on your doorstep or call. I'll bet you get so many orders; your voicemail will be full."

I snicker at her fretting. "I highly doubt I'll have *so* many orders my voicemail groans at me. I have one order, Marianne. Lisa has us setting up for an empire. It's sweet, but I'm not sure it's totally necessary."

Marianne slams down a book atop the stack, suddenly agitated.

My head snaps up, curious as to her sudden shift in temperament.

"You can't think small, Charlotte. This is a big deal. It's worth aiming high. I'm going to prepare for every person in Sweetwater Falls to place multiple reoccurring orders for your amazing cupcakes." She doesn't look happy or wistful, but like she is actually frustrated with me. "It kills me to see you serving stupid food and stupid desserts at the diner. We aren't going to assume that this will be a flop. You're too talented for that."

I set the book down and wrap her in a big hug. "You really think all that?"

"Do you assume I would push this hard to make sure you get off the ground if I didn't think you could do this? No one is placing pity orders because we're your friends. They're going to buy your cupcakes over and over because they're good. We're not going to treat your talent as if it's ordinary and deserves a shrug and a dollar. We're putting our foot on the gas with this."

I squeeze her tighter. "I love you. Do you know that?"

"I love you too much to let you aim low with this. Millionaire by the end of the year or bust."

I chuckle at her moxie, loving that she unleashes only when it's to benefit her friend. "Well, I think that's completely reasonable."

"Good. Because Winifred and I printed up a few flyers to advertise for you." She lowers her chin as our embrace ends. "Agnes is actually going out tomorrow morning to hand them out door to door for you." She grimaces. "Don't be mad."

I balk at her plan that's taken off behind my back. "Are you serious? She doesn't need to do that."

"She sure does. If she wants you to be Charlotte the Brave, then when you take a leap into the unknown, she knows she needs to be there to give you the best push she can. Same as Karen and Winifred. Winifred helped me put together the flyers two days ago. She's been passing them out ever since. She ran out, so I'm printing her more. Karen was hoping you could make a few extra cupcakes tomorrow when you bake Lisa's order, so she can distribute samples to various sweet tooths around Sweetwater Falls."

I gape at her. "You've been doing all this while I've been biting my nails, staring at my computer trying to figure out how to set up a website?"

"That's right. We're in this together." She looks me dead in the eye. "You're not going to fail, Charlotte."

"Fail at what?" comes a voice that spooks me off my balance.

Of course my hand doesn't knock only one book off the counter. My arm sweeps the entire stack Marianne's been sorting onto the floor in a flurry of pages. "Oh!" I freeze, my hands over my mouth as I take in the carnage in comparison to the picturesque man standing before me. "Logan!"

Marianne bursts into fits of giggles, gripping the edge of the counter. "Yes! It's my favorite TV show: The Charlotte and Logan

Hour. He only said three words and you... and then the books..."
She bends in half, holding her stomach while she laughs. "I
have to pee!"

My face is so red, I am certain my cheeks now match my lip
gloss. "I'm sorry! I wrecked your piles!"

Marianne is on her knees now, breaking the universally
understood "be quiet" rule that all libraries adhere to as her
laughter carries through the corridor. "And you say his name
like he's a serial killer and you're a starlet in a black and white
movie!" She clutches at imaginary pearls. "'Logan!'"

My crush gapes at how quickly I can make a mess when he
comes into view. "Wow. That's got to be the fastest disaster I've
ever caused. Are you okay?" He trots around the circulation desk
and gets on his knees. "It's my fault. I spooked you."

His kindness is the worst. If only he had a wretched personality, then I could get over his strikingly handsome features.

I kneel down, horrified that I messed up Marianne's neat
piles, and even more chagrinned that Logan witnessed it all. But
when I lean forward to gather up some of the books, my forehead knocks to Logan's, because of course it does.

"Oh!" I cradle my forehead, shocked at my own stupidity.
"I'm sorry!"

Logan rubs his forehead with one hand and cups the back of
my head with the other. "Are you okay, Miss Charlotte? I wasn't
looking where I was putting my head."

"You know this is my fault," I chide us both. "You're being
nice."

Logan's perfect eyebrow raises. "Would you rather I was
mean?"

*Yes. That would make things so much simpler. I could get over you
already.*

But I don't say that aloud. His palm heats the back of my
head as he examines my forehead with care. "I hurt you," I

confess. "And I made a mess. And I'm about to make Marianne pee herself."

Marianne's laugh mutates to a cackle as she tries to stand. "I love it! Logan, you have to come by more often."

Logan offers me a smile laced with gentle kindness. He's so sweet and unassuming; it steals my breath. "Are you alright?"

"I'm..." If he doesn't take his hand off of my head and back up, I might faint. Dimples for days, perfect yet unintimidating musculature and that way about him that makes a girl believe that men can be sweet without agenda.

Logan's thumb lingers on one of my curls. I know I definitely smell like French fry grease. I'm in shorts and a pink t-shirt, nothing near as classy as his nice jeans and hunter green polo. His eyes are bright green. The sight makes me wonder if there has ever been a more gorgeous color in all of nature.

Marianne is standing now, dabbing at her eyes with her sleeve. "I needed that. You two are the best entertainment."

Logan helps me pick up the books, by which I mean I drop my share of the books three more times before Logan gets them all atop the counter once more. I am an absolute klutz around him.

I do my best to sort the books into genres for Marianne. "These were in perfect piles before I made a fool of myself."

Logan lingers behind the desk, watching me work and then joining in once he sees what I'm doing. "Have you taken up a second job at the library, Charlotte? I had a feeling I would find you here."

Marianne grins at us. "Were you hoping to see Charlotte?" Her teasing sing-song tone holds no subtlety.

If my face could turn a darker shade of red, I am sure it would be practically crimson by now.

Logan smirks and brushes his elbow to mine. "I'm always hoping."

It's too much. His mild flirting turns my limbs to a giraffe's, and I knock over a small stack of books all over again.

I rub my forehead, frustrated with myself and completely flustered. "You know you can't say things like that to me! I read into it too much. I'm already out of sorts whenever you come around."

Logan kneels down to retrieve the four books I knocked to the floor. "Well, I'm hoping you read into it that I want to spend time with you again." He stands slowly, meeting my wide eyes with a gaze that's laced with insecurity. "I hope you read into it that I'd like to take you to dinner and a movie, or whatever sounds like a nice date to you."

I know I didn't hear him right. I'm hearing what I want to hear, or what my fantasy life has concocted for my ears. "You like dinner?"

What?

Logan tilts his head to the side at my stupid question as he sets the books atop the counter. "I do. In fact, if you go out to dinner and a movie with me this Friday night, dinner might end up being my very favorite meal. What do you say?"

9

HEAD AND GUT

*L*ogan's eyes hold a measure of insecurity now. He actually looks like there might be a chance any woman in her right mind might turn him down. I cannot imagine he has ever been rejected, or that he has need to waste his time with me when I clearly do not have my act together.

Is it possible Logan Flowers just asked me out on a date?

"Logan, I..."

I'd love to? That's obvious. *I'd be honored?* Too formal. I sound like one of Marianne's classic literature characters.

Instead what pops out of my mouth is an uncouth, "I'm sweating." I cringe at my own stupidity.

Logan's mouth twists into a wry smile, which I can tell he is trying to iron out.

Marianne bursts into fits of giggles all over again. "That's a yes, by the way," she works out on my behalf. "She would love to go out with you." She holds onto the counter, gripping her side while she hiccups through her laughter. "Five o'clock Friday night? You'll pick her up from Winifred's?"

Logan chuckles in Marianne's direction. "Will I actually be

able to talk to her on the date, or will you need to be the translator?"

I jump on the joke as if it's a serious suggestion. "Yes to Friday night, but can we make it a double date? I can't... You know I won't be able to..." I motion between myself and his obvious beauty. I tug at the collar of my t-shirt. "I can't stop sweating!"

Logan softens with compassion instead of poking fun because that's the kind of gentleman he is. "Of course. I didn't mean to be pushy. I was hoping you would have used my phone number that I gave you weeks ago."

Marianne scribbles on a slip of paper, still snatching at breath between her giggles. "This is Charlotte's phone number. You can put it in your phone and label it 'Giant Chicken'. Call her tonight after she showers from sweating so much. She's dying to go on a date with you." When I clear my throat, she adds. "Double date. We'll meet at Charlotte's."

Logan smirks at me and leans in conspiratorially. "Was that really so hard?"

I nod my head, knowing that if I speak, I will only blurt out something more embarrassing.

Logan turns his head toward Marianne, no doubt sensing that I've hit my limit on how much unintelligent mutterings I can utter in a five-minute span. "Marianne, can you point me to the cookbook section? I think it's time I learned what my stove is for."

"Charlotte can show you." When I shoot daggers at her, she shrugs. "What? I have to get these books sorted. Some sweaty hurricane swept in and made a mess of things. And can you grab the flyers from the copier on your way back? I printed out more."

I move from behind the counter, making sure to keep a respectable distance between myself and Logan. I'm worried I might have a clumsy moment and take down the book stacks like a row of dominoes.

Logan shoots me half a smile. "I don't think I've ever seen Marianne laugh as hard as she does when you're around. I've known her since we were kids. Always so serious. You're good for her."

"The feeling is mutual. I didn't have any solid friends when I lived in Chicago. But we hang out at least every other day, if not more often. I love it." It's easier to talk to Logan when the subject is Marianne.

Logan leans in conspiratorially. "Who do you think she'll invite as her date on Friday?"

"No idea. But it had better be someone real. Not like bringing Agnes. She has to bring someone who..."

"Makes her sweat?" Logan supplies, his left cheek dimpling.

I blush all over again. "Oh, hush. I'm embarrassed enough as it is." We pass by the copier on our way to the cookbook section, so I swipe up the stack of pages.

Logan peers at the papers. "Bravery Bakery? What's that?" His gaze flits over the print, gathering more information. "You're starting a bakery business out of your house? That's a great idea."

I don't know what to do with the blatant compliment, so I pretend I didn't hear it. "Lisa Swanson suggested it. She tried one of my cupcakes and asked if she could order a dozen. She's been helping me turn it into a business." I show him the flyer more clearly. "Though, right now it's more my hobby that's turning out to be pretty expensive. Business license, building a website, business cards... It's all adding up for what will prob-ably turn out to be a couple hundred dollars spent to fill one order of a dozen cupcakes. But Marianne is so excited about it. I figure it's a good way to pass the time."

His expression tightens. "Lisa Swanson placed the order? She's helping you with this?"

I nod. "She's been great."

Logan glances around, making sure no one is in earshot. "Be careful, Charlotte. She might not be the best person to be around right now. My dad is..."

I wave off his concern. "I know she's the prime suspect in Jared's murder. But she didn't do it, Logan." Though, if I was being honest with myself, I would admit that there have been a few times the evidence has pointed her way.

The receipt with peanut oil on it and Jared's coincidental peanut allergy have to be just that—a coincidence.

Logan's head tilts to the side. "How can you know that? Dad certainly seems to think she's guilty."

I shrug. "It's a gut thing. Plus, she was with her husband the night of the murder."

Except that she wasn't with Wesley at home for some span of time where she slipped away to buy said peanut oil.

Logan's mouth pulls to the side. I can tell he also doesn't like that her alibi is from her husband, who might easily lie for her. "Can you promise me you'll be careful when you're with her?"

"Careful how?"

"Careful like, if she's actually the killer, you're not in a position where she might easily murder you."

I smirk at him. "I promise I'll make it as difficult to murder me as possible."

"Thanks."

I wish I had complete confidence that Lisa was innocent.

Then it dawns on me that Logan might be able to cure the angst that swirls in my head every so often when I think about Jared's murder.

I lower my voice and lean in. "I know you can't tell me

anything about the case, but can I put something in your head to get it out of my head?"

Logan folds his arms across his chest. "Of course. That goes for crime stuff and personal stuff. I can always listen. What's on your mind, Miss Charlotte?"

Sheesh, he's a good person.

Guilt swarms up in me at leaning toward the evidence and away from my gut. "Lisa gave us a receipt. She wrote out my business plan on the back of it." My teeth worry my lower lip while my want to trust Lisa conflicts with the evidence. "It was a receipt for peanut oil."

Logan doesn't react, listening still as if waiting for the other shoe to drop. "Okay. Tell me why that's got you worried."

I look around to make sure no one is near enough to overhear. "Jared is allergic to peanuts. I was wondering if there was any forensic work done to see if he was actually strangled to death, or if perhaps he'd been given peanut oil." I touch my stomach. "My gut says Lisa is innocent, but my head can't dismiss something like that. I need to know Jared's death had nothing to do with an allergic reaction, otherwise my head will never shut up about it." I look down at my stomach. "When my head and my gut argue, it's taxing."

To his credit, Logan doesn't rush to come to a conclusion without sufficient evidence. "We didn't consider that possibility. I'll make sure to add that fact to the report. Do you have the receipt? I'll need to take a picture of it."

I close my eyes. "It's in my purse. I really like Lisa. I don't want to get her into trouble. I just want to confirm that Jared didn't die of an allergic reaction." I rub my forehead. "I worry I've done the wrong thing."

Logan shakes his head, his shoulders loosening. "Not at all. If she's guilty, she's guilty. If she's innocent, the evidence will prove that. It's officially off your plate and on mine now."

My chin lowers. "Why don't I feel better?"

Logan holds out his hand. "Because you haven't given me any of those flyers. Can I have a few?"

My eyebrows scrunch together at his abrupt switch in subject. "For what?"

"To hand out. You want more customers than just the one, I take it?"

"Well, ideally, but you don't have to do that."

Logan rolls his eyes. "I know I don't *have* to. I *want* to. I enjoyed being your dishwasher, back when you were baking for The Snuggle Inn."

I tilt my chin toward the floor because this whole thing is too much for me. "I liked that, too." My voice lowers as if I am copping to a horrendous crime. "I enjoyed spending time with you."

I keep my eyes on the floor between us. I like the sweetness of his smile, but it's bound to turn me into a monkey on roller skates if he keeps it up.

"Good. Then the next time you get a big order, how about I swing on by to be your dishwasher again?"

My neck shrinks, which I think counts as a nod. I make to hand him a few flyers, but the whole stack slips from my grip and scatters onto the floor. "Oh, sugar!" I cover my face with my hands.

"I got it this time." Logan bends down and picks up the flyers, handing me back the stack, minus half a dozen, which he keeps for himself.

"Thanks. That's the section you wanted. I have to go." I motion toward the aisle of cookbooks, then quite literally run away from him, knowing that if I am near Logan for a second longer, I will never live down my clumsiness.

10

GROCERY DELIVERY

*M*arianne takes the eggs out of the fridge. "I cannot believe your response to 'will you go on a date with me' was 'I'm sweating.' And fair warning: I'm going to come down with a mysterious flu tomorrow night, so I won't be able to double date."

I whirl on Marianne, fixing her with my most serious expression. "Don't you dare."

Marianne rolls her eyes. "Fine, if you really need a chaperone, I'll bring along Winifred to be my date for the evening. We'll slip out early."

I cluck my tongue at her suggestion with a spatula in hand. "Uh-uh. No way. If I'm going to be nervously sweating all Friday night, then you're calling up that lawyer guy who couldn't keep his eyes off you."

Marianne ceases all movement. "Carlos? No. I couldn't. He lives so far away. Two hours. We haven't seen each other in at least a month."

"Two whole hours, which he would happily drive if it meant a date with you."

Marianne blushes. "You don't know that. We talk on the phone still, but there's no point. He lives too far away."

I shake my head. "You want me to take a risk but you're going to feed me excuses why you have to sit on the bench? Nice try."

"How about let's talk about the cupcakes instead. Or global warming. Or politics. Literally anything but the guy I wish I could be with, but can't because he lives so far away." She sets down the sugar from the cupboard. "Did you check the website to see if you got any orders?"

I cast her a dubious look. "I only got the thing up and running this week. I highly doubt anyone's even gone on it yet. Besides, the online order form would have sent any orders to my email."

"When is the last time you checked your email?"

I shrug. "I dunno. Last week?"

Marianne scoffs at my blasé attitude. "Are you kidding me? Check your email. I bet you got a thousand new orders."

"I bet I got zero, but I love your optimism. You get an A+ on the best friend scale."

Marianne shakes her fists in the air in mock celebration at achieving a perfect friend score. Then she drops the dance. "But seriously. Before we start baking, check your email. It's easier to double the recipe than it is to make two separate orders."

I sigh, knowing that when I check my email, there will be nothing but spam. I pull out my phone and open the email app while Marianne continues getting out the ingredients we'll need to use. I love that we've baked together so many times that she knows what we'll be using without me having to tell her.

My eyes bug. "This can't be right. Hold on. I think I set up the contact form on the website incorrectly. It's probably sending me multiples of the same email, or these are all just a test or something."

Marianne bobs on the balls of her feet, squealing with giddy delight. "I told you! The Live Forever Club has been handing out flyers like crazy. There's no way you don't have a ton of orders."

My stomach drops. "Marianne, this isn't... I don't know how..." I open email after email, each one from a different person in Sweetwater Falls. "A dozen assorted from Delia? Two dozen from Fisher?" I shake my head. "He's just being nice. Why would he order two dozen cupcakes?"

"Because you're a genius in the kitchen!" Marianne practically shouts at me. "Keep reading!"

I scroll through the emails, getting flustered after the first four. "I need to write these down and figure out if I have enough ingredients. I know I don't have enough butter for all of these."

"I'll take care of that. I have a delivery service that can drop off whatever we need."

I sit down, my cheeks hot as explosions go off in my brain. "Is this real? Marianne, there are twenty emails of people placing orders. Oh my goodness. How did this happen?"

Marianne looks like she's about ten seconds away from either throwing a spontaneous party or wringing my neck. "It happened because people got a taste of your talent when you donated all of your cupcakes for the bake sale to help raise funds for the library. It happened because people tasted your cupcakes at the restaurants they used to be sold at, and they sorely miss them. It happened because your only competition is Bill's crummy freezer pies, and *you* are the superior baker!"

The garage door groans, letting us know that Winifred is home. "She's bringing home a new rake and some soil for the garden. She'll need help with that."

I make to stand to assist my great aunt, but Marianne sits me back down. "You make a list of all the orders and take inventory of any extra ingredients we'll need delivered. I'll help Winifred."

The paper fills up with twenty orders, some with two or three dozen. When I finish with my list, my stomach drops.

"Twenty-seven dozen cupcakes," I say to Marianne when she comes back in with Aunt Winnie. "We have to make twenty-seven dozen cupcakes, and that's not counting the dozen we're making for Lisa. So twenty-eight dozen. That's... three-hundred-thirty-six cupcakes. Plus extra for Karen to pass out as free samples."

Marianne screams with delight while Aunt Winifred starts dancing, her hands raised in the air. "That's my girl!"

I fan myself with the list, one step away from pure panic. "We have to shut it down! I can't make that many cupcakes!"

Aunt Winnie's dance stops abruptly. "You can absolutely do this. You can do even more than this if more orders roll in. They paid when they set the orders, right?"

I nod, scared that I took money from people. Even though that's the premise of any business, it feels surreal, and like they might not realize it's me they bought from. I'm no one. And they're not buying something flashy. It's a cupcake.

Marianne and Aunt Winifred gather me up in a hug that squishes me from both sides. Aunt Winnie kisses my cheek. "You have the money to get more ingredients because they prepaid. You have the time to bake because you've got all night, and the orders aren't set to be picked up until tomorrow. This is good, honey cake. It's real good."

I don't know why I'm scared. Tears shouldn't be rolling down my cheeks right now. This is the part where I'm supposed to be deliriously happy. And maybe that's exactly what I am. But it's measured with an unhealthy dose of fear. What if I fail? What if I burn several batches of cupcakes? What if there aren't enough hours in the evening to bake them all, and I don't get an order filled?

The storm of worry that rises up in me threatens to burble out of my mouth, but when Aunt Winifred's soft lips kiss my cheek a second time, I remember to breathe. "I'm so proud of you! Even if you had just the one order, you did it! This is your dream, and you're doing it!"

"Is it supposed to feel this scary? Like I'm going to cry and barf at the same time?"

Marianne and Winifred nod in unison. "Yes," they reply together.

Aunt Winnie caresses my curls. "Only the best things in life feel like that. If you weren't a little nervous, I would say you didn't have your head in the game."

Marianne twines her fingers through mine. "One step at a time. Let's make a list of ingredients we're going to be short on, and I'll send for them."

Aunt Winifred nods. "That's good. One foot in front of the other. Slow at first, and then before you know it, you're sprinting." She pinches my cheek. "My little business owner!"

The urge to vomit is keen in my stomach, but I follow Marianne's lead and sit back down. She situates her chair beside mine as we make the grocery list together. Then she types it into her phone, presumably into some sort of shipping app while I start creaming the wet ingredients. I didn't realize Sweetwater Falls had anything like that set up for grocery delivery.

My brain is firing in fits and spurts, adding up the amount of butter needed to make the s'mores cupcakes that were ordered. "I'm so grateful I took Lisa's advice and kept the menu simple. Four flavors means I'm not having to make an odd batch of just one kind."

Marianne nods and then sets down her phone. "The rest of the ingredients will be here within the hour. I'll start sifting together the dry ingredients. Which flavor are you making right now?"

"S'mores. That's a chocolate cupcake with a melty chocolate bomb inside. Toasted marshmallow frosting with a graham cracker crumble on top."

Marianne grins. "Perfect. I love that one. I still think you should put one of your wild flavors on the menu. Like, have your standard four flavors, but then a flavor of the month or something. I love all your cupcakes, but your wild ones are so cool."

I chuckle at her enthusiasm. "Cool, yes, but Sweetwater Falls hasn't fallen in love with the wild flavors yet. They like desserts they've heard of. Double fudge. S'mores. Things like that."

"Hmm. I still think my idea is awesome."

"It is. Let's see if we make it through tonight, and then we'll think about adding a flavor of the month."

"Excellent."

The two of us have baked in this kitchen so many times; the whole thing is like a dance. I'm anxious for the groceries to arrive, but we have enough to knock out cupcake after cupcake until they get here. The name of the game is to get the cupcakes in the oven. I work on the batter while Marianne whips the toasted marshmallow frosting.

"We really need another mixer," Marianne complains. "Or one with a bigger bowl. I can't make the amount we need in this, or it will overflow. Boo." She juts out her lower lip while the egg whites are whipped into a frenzy. "Hand me that pen and paper?"

I slide the items her way while I start bringing together the next round of cupcakes.

Marianne thinks aloud while she writes. "We'll need bigger mixers. A few more cupcake pans. You have two of the twenty-four cupcake pans, but you need two more, so we can get the next batch ready to go while the others are in there."

I shake my head. "All of that stuff is expensive."

Marianne pauses, tilting her head to the side. "Charlotte, what's the cost of a dozen cupcakes on the website?"

I rattle off the number she insisted we charge.

"Okay, multiply that by twenty-eight."

My eyes widen and the spatula slips out of my hand. "Oh my goodness. We might be able to buy everything we need this month."

Marianne grins at me when the doorbell rings. "If the orders keep coming in, you'll be able to buy all you need to make this a formidable operation tomorrow." Marianne kisses my cheek as she flits toward the front room to answer the door. "That'll be the groceries."

Success never occurred to me. This was supposed to be my hobby that I did mostly to feed my soul and convince the Live Forever Club that they hadn't made a mistake in dubbing me "Charlotte the Brave". But people are actually ordering my cupcakes.

I pause scooping the batter into the liners because I cannot fend off the tears of gratitude any longer.

Lisa took a chance on me. She pushed through her grief and saw my dream clearly, and then helped me pursue it.

Marianne is giving up her evening so she can bake like a madwoman with me. She believed in this business before it was even off the ground.

Aunt Winifred and the cuties of the Live Forever Club have been handing out flyers, advertising my cupcakes for me. They did all they could to give my business a fighting chance, and all without being asked.

I never had true friends before moving to Sweetwater Falls.

Tears pool and cascade down my cheeks when I try to blink them away. My lower lip quivers. My soul fills with love and appreciation for this sweet town who opened their arms to me, and now their wallets.

I pull a tissue from my pocket and dab at my eyes.

Marianne calls to me from the front room. "Charlotte, are you holding anything?"

"Just a tissue. If I make it through the next batch without crying, I think I deserve a reward."

Heavy footsteps meet me in the kitchen. "Why are you crying?"

Before I can stop myself, a shriek rips from my lips. "Logan!"

Marianne bursts into laughter. "You did it again! You say his name like he just walked in on you in the bathroom. I wanted to make sure you weren't holding a mixing bowl or something, because I didn't want you to drop the batter all over the floor when you saw our reinforcements."

"Our what?" I sniffle and swipe at the moisture on my cheeks again.

"Logan is our grocery delivery man." Marianne slaps his shoulder.

Logan sets an armload of groceries on the small bare spot on the counter. "That's right. I'm your delivery man, and now I'm going to be your dishwasher. You know that's my forte." After he frees himself of the groceries, Logan closes the gap between us. He doesn't give my nerves a chance to overtake me but gathers me in a hug that squeezes more tears from my eyes. "What's wrong?"

My forehead finds its way to the crook of his neck so I can bury my tears in his shirt. "Nothing's wrong at all. I'm happy. Overwhelmed, maybe. I didn't think anyone would place orders, but twenty-eight dozen, Logan!" His name sounds strange on my tongue. "Twenty-eight dozen cupcakes."

"That's amazing." His reply is gentle, his voice coated in sweetness without sounding pandering. "And completely unsurprising. You're talented, Charlotte." When I lean back to look up at him to gage the sincerity on his face, measuring it against the honesty in his voice, he smiles down at me. His hand smooths across my back. "You're talented, and you're not alone."

My knees weaken when he leans in. He brushes his nose

across mine in manner so delicate, I worry my helpless whimper might have come out as a moan.

Then Logan does something so precious, I am certain I am imagining the sweetness. He lifts his chin and kisses the tip of my nose. "Now if you'll excuse me, Miss Charlotte, I've got some dishes to wash."

Though my knees are weak and my brain pure mush, I manage to find my way back to the mixing bowl. I stare at the ingredients until Marianne gives me a nudge in the right direction.

"Can I borrow your cell phone?" I ask Marianne. "I need to call Aunt Winnie, and my phone is almost out of juice."

Marianne hands over her device.

I pretend that the noise from the sink and the mixer is too loud, so I move into the living room, scrolling past my aunt's name until I land on Carlos. Their call history has me smiling. They talk nearly every night on the phone, sometimes for an hour at a time.

If Marianne gets to spring my crush on me, then I get to return the favor. Marianne might be planning to bring Aunt Winnie as her date on Friday night, but she's going to get a little surprise all her own.

That's right; two can play at this game.

After I make the quick call, I cannot keep the grin off my face.

If this is what life is like in Sweetwater Falls, then this perfect small town has earned a permanent place in my heart.

11

BEARER OF BAD NEWS

I don't offer delivery for my cupcake business, which is just as well. I have a day job I had to wake up before dawn to get to, thanks to Bill changing my shift around. Aunt Winnie offered to manage the pickups, since she didn't have plans to leave the house until the afternoon.

This cannot be my long-term plan.

Though Aunt Winnie assured me she didn't mind, I don't like the idea of taking over her kitchen, and then her whole Friday morning.

Logan's text this morning dances in my mind. "Good morning, Cupcake Queen."

It was simple, cute and made me smile. In fact, I haven't stopped smiling about it all morning. I do my best to put it out of my mind, quite aware that even the thought of Logan might send me headfirst into another clumsy moment.

The diner has a decent flow going, though it's not quite as hectic as it was last week when news of the murder was fresh in everyone's minds.

When Lisa walks in, I'm grateful there are a few open seats in my section.

I greet her with a hug. "I'm so glad you came in today. I have questions. Business questions." Then a grin takes me over. "I love that I can say that! What can I get you this morning?"

Lisa casts a faint smile up at me, and for the first time, I see dark circles under her eyes. "Hammer to the head? Is there a bowl of something on this menu that could fix my life?"

I frown, sitting down in the booth across from her. "What's wrong, Lisa?"

"They still don't have another suspect for Jared's murder, so Sheriff Flowers keeps circling back to me. I don't have any other proof that I didn't leave the house when we left the fair and came home, other than Wesley's word. I have no idea how to get Sheriff Flowers off my back. It's hard enough to deal with the death of a friend and business partner, but to be hounded by the cops on top of it?" She digs her knuckles into her temples. "I'm already the town's loose woman. To be a murderer on top of it is just overkill." Then she snorts at her phrasing. "They can call me The Overkiller."

I set down my order pad and reach across the table to rest my hand on her wrist. "This will pass. Not right now, and maybe not soon, but it will pass. Have you been back to the gym yet?"

Lisa sniffles as her eyes pool with moisture. "I can't go. Can you imagine? I'm accused of Jared's murder. I'm afraid they won't let me in."

Compassion washes over me. "Of course they'll let you in! That's silly talk." I shake my head. "You're dealing with so much."

"Ate half a pint of that low-cal non-dairy ice cream last night. Now I'm sad *and* I have a stomachache."

My face twitches with disdain. "That stuff won't do you a lick of good. The cupcakes you ordered are at the house now. After you get some food in your belly, go pick up your cupcakes and grieve nice and proper—with sugar and fat and dairy."

Lisa chuckles at what she thinks is a joke, but I couldn't be more serious. If I had to drown my sorrows in something that tasted like the carton it came in, I would be in tears the next day, too.

Lisa swipes at her eyes and then waves her hand like she wants to clear the air of her grief. "I'm so proud of you for tackling that to-do list and getting your business going so quickly."

"Well, I had help. Marianne loves herself a good to-do list."

"You'd be surprised how many people beg for a plan but then don't bother to consult it or even take the first step on the list. I stand by my assessment: I'm proud of you. Before you know it, you'll have multiple orders coming in."

I'm not sure if I'm allowed to smile while she still has tears on her cheeks, so I keep my merriment muted as best I can. "Actually, the website has only been up a couple days, and I've already had multiple orders! I was baking until eleven o'clock last night to get them all finished."

Lisa perks up. "That's incredible! See? I told you this would work."

"Thanks to your plan."

"Thanks to your cupcakes."

We giggle at our mutual inability to take a compliment without syphoning some of the glory onto others.

"Good that you're set up to only fill orders two days a week, otherwise you would be baking every night. You've got this, Charlotte. I'll bet you make your startup cost back by the end of the week."

My shoulders fall. I know I'm ignoring my tables, but I don't want to leave her just yet. "Lisa, I know this isn't the right time, but I'm not sure when the right time might be. Maybe you can talk to a lawyer if I tell you this sooner rather than later."

Lisa sits up straighter, her tears coming to a stop. "I'm listening."

"When I went to pick up your yoga mat from your gym, I met a man there and we started talking about Jared. He was one of Jared's clients, too."

Lisa nods. "Jared was pretty high in demand. He got results."

I roll my tongue around the inside of my teeth, fishing for the right words. "He was also one of Jared's investors."

Lisa stills. "Jared had other investors? I don't think that's true. Jared told Wesley and me that we were the only ones. That's why he kept asking for more money."

I hate being the bearer of bad news. "The guy said he invested five thousand dollars, which was the buy-in, but Jared recently asked him for more money. The guy said he knew of at least half a dozen of other people who also invested the same amount."

Lisa pales. "That's not possible. He said we were the only people putting anything into the business. Over and over, he begged us for more money because we were the only ones pushing his business forward."

"I hate that you're out ten thousand dollars."

Lisa drops her head. "Can you keep a secret?"

A feeling of dread sweeps over me. "What happened?"

"I didn't tell Wesley, but I took a thousand dollars of my own and gave it to Jared. So we're actually out eleven thousand dollars. I knew my husband would say no, and Jared really needed it. He wanted to get a lease on a place, but he didn't have enough. We lost a great piece of property because I couldn't come up with more."

I close my eyes so I don't have to see the brutal impact of my words when they land. "The guy I met at the gym was upset with himself, just like you, because he lost a friend, sure, but he also lost all that money. When Jared asked him for more, Jared told him that he'd already located a space for the new gym, but that it needed some fixing up still."

Lisa's words come out slowly, and through gritted teeth. "Jared told us that he didn't have a building yet. That was two days before he died. That's the last time we saw him alive. So unless he found a building the day before he died..."

I purse my lips. "I thought you might want that information in case you were going to try to get your money back somehow. No idea if that's possible, but you deserve to know." I hang my head. "I'm sorry I'm telling you these things! I'm like, walking bad news for you. I promise that the next time we see each other, I will only have happy things to talk about."

Lisa's hand on mine is most welcome. "You were right to tell me this. Thank you. I'll talk to Wesley tonight."

A flicker of an idea occurs to me, but I realize I might need help. "Do you have a guest pass for your gym? I want to talk to him again. Ivan is his name. I have more questions."

"Sure. I'll drop one off at your house when I pick up the cupcakes. What are you hoping to find out?"

"I want to see how far this thing goes. It might give you closure to see the building Jared secured."

"You don't have to do that."

"I want to. I'm breaking your heart all over the place. Please let me help."

"Well, okay." She leans back in the booth. "I admit, it would be nice to see the building, if there even is one."

"I'm sure there is. I'll find it, and maybe that will take some of the sting out of the whole thing."

I stand up and make a show of kissing the top of her head, so people know she is my friend, and she is nothing like a loose woman or a killer.

At least, I hope she's not the killer.

I go back to waiting tables, praying that I didn't just make Lisa's life infinitely worse.

I need to fix this.

WORKING OUT THE TRUTH

I cannot recall the last time I was in a gym. I think I had a brief bout of fancying myself a runner for a month or two in college, but other than that, I'm a girl who mostly enjoys going for walks as exercise.

Do I want to be up two hours before my breakfast shift at the diner starts? No. But this is when Ivan mentioned he prefers to work out, so here I am in what I hope looks like gym attire, but is really just pink sweatpants and a white t-shirt.

I'm sure I stand out when I check in at the front desk with the guest pass Lisa gave me.

Did I think my plan through? Not really, or not enough. If Ivan isn't here, then I just wasted Lisa's guest pass. I didn't get the man's last name, either. There might be more than one Ivan. Plus, he might want to be left alone, if he even is here. He comes here before dawn so he can get a good workout in. Judging by the thickness of his neck, I'm guessing he doesn't prefer to be interrupted during his gym time.

Still, I have to know. Why I don't just butt out and stick to cupcakes and waitressing is beyond me. But I don't like to see my friend fleeced, which, if she didn't murder Jared, she doesn't deserve.

I don't expect to see Ivan on the treadmills, nor hanging around the yoga studio. The gym is huge, and despite the early hour, there are quite a few people on the machines, though it isn't anywhere near as packed as it was when I visited this gym before.

My visions of the insides of gyms range from the leotard-clad eighties movies all the way to muscle-bound weightlifters who throw the weights down and shout their aggressive glee with a guttural growl.

Fortunately, this is nothing like that. Most people in here are focused on their workouts with earbuds on and determination on their faces.

Including Ivan, whom I spot in the corner by the... I'm not sure exactly what that contraption is. It looks like a tall jungle gym for weightlifters. I am not touching that. Not a great idea to have a clumsy moment near that thing.

I'm careful with my steps, making sure I don't trip over anything or anyone as I make my way to Ivan. He doesn't see me at first; his focus is solely on his reflection. I have no idea how many pounds Ivan is curling, but it looks heavy enough that I make sure I don't interrupt his reps.

That's right. I know the word "reps".

Ivan's tank top is tight and shredded on both sides, exposing his barreled ribcage in case... in case his stomach needs proper ventilation?

When he finally sets down the weights, I approach him with all the politeness of a flight attendant. "Excuse me, Ivan?"

Ivan has to turn his shoulders instead of just his chin because his neck is so thick. His serious expression mutates into a smile when recognition pings on his features. "Charlotte? I was wondering if I'd see you again."

"Lucky me, I tracked you down. Could I interrupt your workout for two minutes?"

He motions to the weights, as if he thinks I mean to cut in and use his gear. "By all means."

"I'm not here for the workout. I got a guest pass from a friend so I could find you." I cringe at how forward I sound. But I know Ivan likes a quiet, uninterrupted workout, so I do my best to speed through the distraction so he can get back to enjoying his morning, if that's what it is he's doing.

Ivan tilts his head to the side. "I'm intrigued. What can I do for you in two minutes?"

I fiddle with the hem of my shirt, suddenly realizing how very out of my element I am. I didn't take chances in Chicago, but after a few months in Sweetwater Falls, I'm digging to the bottom of a scandal in my free time. My, how I've grown.

Or perhaps I've changed for the worse, involving myself in scandals that have nothing to do with me.

Either way, I'm here and it's too late to back out now. "You're not going to like the subject," I warn him, my hands up in surrender. "I wanted to know if I could get the address Jared sent you. The one for the new gym he was going to open."

Ivan's expression tightens. "It's not going to do you much good now."

"I figured. I wanted to check out the space. The friend of mine who invested was shocked to learn he had a building. Jared told her that he needed more money before he could get one. I thought it might give her some closure to see the building she invested in. She's a little flummoxed that Jared didn't tell her he'd secured a building."

Ivan's head hangs, and instantly I feel terrible. That was too much information I gave him, wrecking his day for no good reason. I came here for the address, not to ruin his morning.

"Jared only told me because I made him."

My words come out slow and higher pitched. "How does one do that, exactly?"

He motions to his physique. "I backed him into a corner in the locker room one day. Scared him a little. Nothing too rough. Just a bit of a shakeup." He shrinks at the horror on my face. "I'm not proud of it. But I'm out five grand and the little punk kept asking for more. So I demanded answers and progress, and the next day, he came back with an address."

I fix Ivan with a stern look, which is laughable, given that he could throw me across the gym like a ragdoll. "Ivan, I would never think you the type to solve your problems with violence."

He seems to shrink under the weight of my scolding. "Neither would I. It turns out, I'm not built to be an investor. It doesn't bring out the best in me." He lowers his chin. "Would it help if I told you I was sorry?"

"It would help if you never did anything like that ever again."

He places his right hand over his heart. "Yes, ma'am. You wanted the address, right? For your friend?"

"That would be helpful, yes. See how that works? I asked you for the address without needing to corner you in a locker room."

"Yeah, yeah. Your way is better. Hold on." He fishes out his phone and flips through the screen. "You ready?"

I pull out my phone and take down the address. "Thank you, Ivan. I'm so sorry this happened to you—losing a friend and losing the money."

Ivan waves off my condolences. "Did you need a spot?"

I glance around at the equipment. "Oh, no. I only used a guest pass so I could get my friend the address. I don't actually know how to use any of this stuff."

Ivan motions for me to follow him to a bench with two hooks raised on either side of the end. "You're helping a friend; I'll help you. A little tutorial so this place doesn't seem so over-whelming. You've got that deer in headlights look about you."

I grimace at the prospect of lifting anything heavier than a full mixing bowl. "I don't know. I'm pretty sure this part of the gym is for people who know what they're doing."

Ivan brushes off my concern. "Common misconception. And because I *do* know what I'm doing, I'll make sure you don't hurt yourself. It's therapeutic to lift weights when life spins out of control." He demonstrates how to position oneself on the bench and then stands so I can follow his lead.

This is not what I came here to do.

Though, I suppose I did use a guest pass, so it's not as if I'm not allowed to try it.

Almost as if Aunt Winifred is with me in all of her ninety-one-year-old glory, I feel her push me forward, reminding me that I am Charlotte the Brave. I can try new things without being this afraid.

I draw in a steadying breath before I rest my back atop the bench, positioning my shoulders between the two raised hooks.

Ivan moves over to a rack of different sized discs, picking two small ones and screwing them on either end of the bar.

Images of me not being able to lift it at all swarm in my head. Then cartoonish depictions of the bar falling on my neck and crushing my windpipe haunt my brain.

I'm about to tell Ivan that I can't do this, but he's already resting the bar across the raised hooks. He stands near my head and looks down at me. He doesn't smile exactly, but his nod is reassuring. "Okay, so fix your hands here. We're going to lift and then bring it down almost to your chest. Then back up."

"What if I drop it?"

The corner of his mouth quirks. "That's why you have a spotter. I'll make sure you don't hurt yourself."

I want to warn him of my clumsy inclinations, but as Logan is nowhere near this gym, I should be able to follow simple instructions without hurting myself.

I bite down on my lower lip as I lift the bar and then slowly bring it down toward my chest. When I hoist it back up, Ivan is ready with praise as if I'm five years old attempting to ride a bike without training wheels for the first time. "See? That's good, Charlotte. Let's do it again. Is the weight okay?"

"It's not as heavy as I thought it would be."

"It doesn't need to be heavy for your first time trying this out. You want to get the motion down, the pace of it all, otherwise you'll add more weight prematurely and injure yourself."

I take in his advice and keep at it. He counts out twelve repetitions, and then declares me ready for a new machine.

"How did that feel?"

I grin at him as I sit up. "I'm kinda proud of myself. I tried something new and nothing bad happened."

Ivan chuckles. "That's usually how it goes. The fear of the thing is worse than the thing itself."

I let his wisdom sink in as we move to the next contraption, and the next. We fall into a companionable rhythm of him demonstrating an exercise and then me doing my best to keep up. At the end of the hour, we go for a nice walk on the treadmills together. We are the only people talking in the entire gym, as almost everyone else is wearing headphones and keeping to themselves.

When I know my time is just about up because I'll need to go to work soon, we indulge in a sweaty hug before we part, this time exchanging phone numbers so we can hang out if I'm ever in the area again.

I'm so proud of myself for trying something different and being brave. I made a new friend, which is just about the best feeling in the world.

I don't have the time or clean clothes, so I don't bother with a shower. Instead I walk out the door and drive straight for the address Ivan gave me.

Part of me hopes that Jared wasn't a scammer, intent on schmoozing money from people with no intention of making good on his word. I hope I pull into the parking lot of a building that could have been a glorious gym. Lisa is adept at making business plans. Perhaps she can somehow get her money back and invest in the dream Jared sold her. Maybe she can make this into the gym she wanted to see come to life.

My stomach sinks when I pull into the small parking lot my GPS leads me to. I doublecheck the address, hoping I've gotten it wrong.

Though Marianne is working, I call her cell phone because I need to share this information with someone. The second the call connects, I lay out the bad news. "Marianne, I got the address from Ivan of the gym Jared had them investing in. He told Ivan he got a building, remember?"

Marianne gets her head in the game in a flash because she's that good. "I remember. Jared told Lisa he needed more money to secure a lease, but Ivan had been told he'd just made a payment on a building for their new gym."

"I'm there right now. I'm in the parking lot of the address where the new gym is supposed to be."

I can practically hear the frown in Marianne's voice. "You're what? We always go on these adventures together! Don't you dare solve the puzzle without me!"

I snicker at her indignation. "You're working, Marianne. And believe me, the mystery is far from solved. I'm in the parking lot of Jared's new gym, only there's one giant problem."

"What's that?"

"There's no way this building could ever be a gym. It's a tiny fast-food joint, and it's open for business. It hasn't been sold. Looks like there are barely five tables are in the dining area. And the parking lot only has a dozen spaces." I glance down the street on either side. "And there isn't enough real estate to build onto the fast-food place, if Jared was thinking of buying it and somehow making it bigger. There just isn't room. It backs up to an alley."

Marianne gasps, her horror mirroring mine. "Jared lied. There wasn't any business for the investors. They were only lining his pockets. He never had any intention of opening a gym for them. He was taking their money and feeding them lies."

The wretched truth rings through my car. "My thoughts exactly. I have to tell Lisa. If she can get a good lawyer, maybe she can get some of her money back. I don't exactly know how all of that works, but she doesn't deserve to lose that much money because Jared fleeced her. Ivan and the others, too."

Marianne swallows hard. "I might know a lawyer who can at least point us in the right direction."

Her suggestion is the only thing that breaks me from my angst. "Can you call Carlos?" My tenor switches to a slight tease directed at Marianne. "That is, if you have his number."

I know she does. She talks to him nearly every day. Even though he lives two hours away, when he came into Sweetwater Falls a while back to take care of some lawyerly business, the two were clearly smitten with each other.

Marianne ignores the tease in my tone. "Of course I'll call him. Anything to help Lisa."

"Thanks, Marianne." I sober, watching the employees through the window go about their normal workday. "And hey, next time I go to a tiny fast-food joint for investigative purposes, I'll make sure to force you to come with me."

"You'd better."

When I end the call, I know the next person I talk to about this needs to be Lisa.

I am not looking forward to that conversation.

13

CHARLOTTE THE CHICKEN

*W*orking at a greasy diner after working out without a shower in between is just about the most disgusting thing one can do (except for maybe participating in a manure snowball fight), but I manage to get through my shift without grossing my customers out too much. I've got ten minutes left on the clock and my mind is already focusing on the yardwork that needs to be done around the house. Winifred used to pay one of the locals to do it all for her, but since I live there now, I've taken over most of the outdoor yardwork to help out.

She shoots me a text to please pick up a dozen rolls of toilet paper on my way home. I oblige, swallowing the urge to apologize to the redheaded store clerk for my unkempt appearance at the Colonel's General store when I check out with the toilet paper.

I'm pretty sure we have more than enough at the house, but whatever. I like running little errands for Aunt Winnie. Makes me feel like we're part of a team.

When I get home, Aunt Winifred tends her garden while I mow the lawn and trim the bushes. It's become our weekly routine that I look forward to, if only because I need a little sunshine on my skin. I don't bother showering when I get home but dive straight into the yardwork. Exercising before dawn and facing something that intimidated me gives me renewed vigor as I maneuver the mower around the gorgeous landscaping. I've been caring for every inch of the yard over the past couple of months.

Plus, the yardwork gives me plenty of time to consider the double date that's scheduled for tonight.

I need to bow out. I was going to before I started mowing the lawn, but I couldn't find my phone. I'll stay home and munch on popcorn with Aunt Winnie while she crochets another doily.

There's no risk involved in that.

I love Sweetwater Falls. Though the convenience of apartment life back in Chicago was nice, I'll admit, there is something satisfying about cutting your own grass and working up a good sweat in the name of taking pride in one's home.

It's nice to work near Aunt Winifred while she gardens. I even brought out Buttercream—my precious little goldfish that Logan won me at the Twinkle Lights Festival back when I was new in town.

Though, I'm still mostly addressed as "new girl" by most.

Buttercream swims in the bowl, blinking at the change in scenery as I go back and forth behind the mower.

If anyone was in more desperate need of a shower, I would like to meet said person, because I'm sure my deodorant has given up the good fight by now.

The double date is scheduled to go down in less than an hour. No matter how much I try to reframe the evening as four people hanging out, I still know there is no way I can go through with the night as planned. To picture me on a date with Logan sends my brain short-circuiting. It doesn't compute. Even the happy idea of Marianne being surprised with Carlos showing up as her date doesn't give me the bravery I need not to chicken out.

I have to cancel. Marianne and Carlos can go out together and have a lovely time. I don't want to embarrass myself in front of Logan. Marianne pushed him into asking me out. He didn't want to go, I'll bet; he was just being polite.

Where on earth is my phone?

When the lawn is finished and the clippings are swept off the path, I set all the tools back in the garage in their proper spot. Then I move into the house to pour myself and Winifred two tall glasses of her special homemade dragon fruit lemonade. I cast around for my phone, but I haven't seen it since shortly after I finished my shift. I swear I put it on the counter, but it's not there.

I bring Winifred a glass of lemonade, insisting she take a break.

"Oh, you, always looking after me," Aunt Winnie says as she takes the glass, pulling off her gloves and setting them in the dirt. "Thanks, honey cake." She takes a sip. "Oh, that's refreshing."

"So good." I organize the packets of seeds in alphabetical order while we rest together under the sunshine. I think I've spent a few too many days at the library in my spare time if alphabetizing is the first thing that occurs to me to do when there is mild disorder.

"You might want to get ready for your double date, honey. Isn't it happening soon?"

I nod. "I can't find my phone. I was going to text Logan to cancel. Marianne can enjoy her surprise date with Carlos. I like that plan far better."

Though she's just had lemonade, this is the thing that makes her expression sour. "Charlotte McKay, I can't believe I'm hearing this. Why are you intending on cancelling with that sweet boy?"

I love that she calls Logan a boy, even though he's thirty-five years old. I stare into my half-drained drink. "He only said okay to going because Marianne strong-armed him into it. Besides, you know I'll make a fool of myself. How would you feel if Humphry Bogart came to life and asked you on a date? It's too grand. He's too beautiful. I've had a long day, and I don't want to end it feeling like an idiot."

Winifred shakes her head at me. "What's your name again?"

"Charlotte," I reply, unsure what she's getting at.

"No, it's Charlotte the Brave. You're a risk-taker. You're a beauty and Logan is smart enough to spot the obvious. The boy is smitten."

My cheeks flush. "He is not. He's polite. He's a nice person."

"He volunteered to come by twice a week to wash your dishes. He's smitten."

"Again, no. He's nice. And either way, the whole thing is a bad idea. I'm not ready to humiliate myself, playing a game I know I'm no good at. I'm not great at dating in general. I don't want that trend to follow me here."

Winifred takes a long sip, keeping her eyes from me. "Pity you can't find your phone. I'm not sure how you're going to chicken out and cancel a perfectly good date without a phone."

I still, and then slowly turn my head toward her. "Aunt Winifred, what do you know about my phone?"

"I know you left it on the counter." She motions to my gold-fish who is swimming in its bowl in the bright sunshine. "I think Buttercream made off with your phone. Had a feeling you might self-sabotage." When my mouth pops open at her mischievous behavior, Winifred lifts her chin. "It's one thing to be brave some of the time, taking a bold step here and there. That's all well and good, but then to take that forward momentum and throw it away because you feel undeserving? I won't stand for it."

"Winifred, I need my phone."

"Do you? Because I don't think you can make phone calls in the shower, which is where you need to be right now if you're going to be semi-presentable for your date."

I guffaw at her moxie. "Are you serious?"

"Serious and certain that you are not going to stand up that sweet boy. What's he done to deserve that?"

I stammer over her phrasing. "You know it's not like that. I'm letting him out of an obligation he doesn't want to do. I'm sure he'll be relieved."

Winifred fumbles a bit in her attempt to stand, so I pry myself off the dirt and help her up. "Shower. I'll lay out something nice for you to wear. You're not going out in cut-offs and a tank top."

I gape at her, seeing clearly that she's not going to back down. "I thought we could spend the evening together. Watch old movies and enjoy the night just us girls."

Aunt Winnie chuckles, shaking her head. "Oh, no you don't. I'm no one's excuse for not facing their fears. Besides, I have plans with the girls tonight."

"You do not. You're just saying that because you want me to go on this double date."

She raises her nose. "I certainly do. Agnes, Karen and I are going to toilet paper the sheriff's house. It's our annual tradition we just started this year."

I snicker at her childish antics. And actually, I do believe that they have plans to toilet paper Sheriff Flowers' home. That sort of ridiculous behavior is right up their alley.

And it explains why she requested me to stop at the Colonel's General store to pick up more toilet paper after work.

Oh, Aunt Winnie.

When I finally hit a wall and see there's no way out, my nerves begin to take over. I tug at my fingers, sweating anew. "You don't understand. I'll say something stupid! I'll drop the popcorn again." I remember back to when Marianne set us up on a double date the first time. It ended exactly like that, with Logan leaving early for a work emergency.

"Then the popcorn gets dropped. You'll both have a good laugh, and you'll enjoy the rest of the movie. He's a good man, honey cake. He's worth the risk of looking foolish." She points at my anxiety-laced mannerisms. "And by the way, you're worth that risk, too. Your happiness is worth a little sweat. All of the amazing things in life are."

I can't argue her valid points, but the urge to whine is strong.

Before I can devolve into a complete child, Aunt Winnie points toward the house. "March. I'll see if Buttercream can locate your phone when Logan gets here. Mischievous fish."

I march up the stairs to the bathroom down the hall from my bedroom, unsure how I lost the upper hand in that exchange so quickly. My shower takes far longer than it normally would, partly because I'm hoping that Logan shows up and then leaves because I'm not ready yet.

When a shot of icy water pelts me out of nowhere, I scream. "Winifred, did you flush the toilet?"

"I sure did," she calls through the wall. "I know what you're doing, wasting time in there. You've got two sweet gentlemen downstairs waiting on you. Time to live up to your name, Charlotte the Brave."

I turn off the tap, shivering as I towel off. I'm very aware that Logan is downstairs. Suddenly my plan to take too long getting ready smacks of rudeness rather than the fear it very much is.

Winifred hands me a blue sundress I don't often have occasion to wear. She fishes under the collar of her shirt and takes off her necklace, clasping it around my neck. "Throw it on, run a comb through your hair, and you're ready to go. If you're not downstairs in three minutes, I'm going to go through your phone and delete all your contacts."

I gape at her threat, which I have no doubt she will not hesitate to make good on.

As soon as she exits, I rush through my routine, snagging my brush through my tangles. I toss the dress over my head and brush my teeth at lightning speed. I don't have time to blow-dry my hair, so it gets wound atop my head in a tight ballerina bun that I hope will pass as sophisticated and not sloppy. I slide my feet into pink ballet flats and race down the stairs, knowing the window for a polite delay in plans is nearly coming to a close.

I'm breathless when I reach the living room, where Winifred has been entertaining Logan and Carlos. The three of them are drinking tea and chuckling together, but that all stops when I come into the room.

Logan stands like a true gentleman straight out of a television show, even though I feel several steps shy of being a proper lady. He nods his head toward me. "Miss Charlotte."

My throat dries. "Logan," is all I can manage to croak out. On the evenings he comes over to wash dishes, it takes more than a few minutes of being around him before I get used to his presence. I have no such cushion right now. It's sink or swim, and I am most definitely sinking.

Logan crosses the room, a tease of a smile quirking his lips as he approaches with a hand behind his back. When he brings his fist out, he presents me with a simple pink rose. "For you. And just so you don't think I'm being too forward, I brought one for Winifred, too."

Aunt Winnie chimes in with a churlish, "Mine was red, so don't get any ideas, Charlotte. Logan fancies me."

Logan and I share a chuckle as I take the rose, smelling the bloom so deeply that my eyes close at the heavenly scent. "It's so pretty. Thank you." Even though we're not alone, it feels like we are the only two people existing in a ten-mile radius. "I'm sorry I kept you waiting," I admit, my words coming out in an uncouth rush. "I don't know what I'm doing. I'm nervous because it's you."

Logan leans in, fixing me with the most beguiling eyes that ever were. "Can I tell you a secret? I don't know what I'm doing, either. I'm nervous, too, because it's *you*."

My breath hitches as I search his face for signs of pity. Instead, I find a sliver of vulnerability mixed in with a smile that holds no cunning or ulterior motive.

When the doorbell rings, Aunt Winnie moves to answer the door, but I stop her before she gets there. "Actually, Carlos, would you mind grabbing the door? That'll be Marianne. I want to see the look on her face when she sees who her date for the evening *really* is."

Carlos chortles as he moves to the front door. He holds no insecurity, wondering if Marianne will be pleased to see that he has been swapped for her original choice in dates. He opens up the door, grinning at what is now a stunned Marianne. "Fancy meeting you here."

Marianne gasps, and then a smile overtakes her entire body. "Carlos? I didn't know you were in town! Why didn't you tell me? What are you doing here?"

Carlos brings Marianne in for a hug, her expression still stunned. "I came into town to take you on a date. Why else would I be here?"

Marianne laughs, breathless at the twist her evening has taken already before it's properly begun. "I'm so happy to see you. How did you..." Then she peeks around his shoulder at me. "Charlotte, did you do this?"

I shrug. "Winifred can't be your date tonight. She's got plans with the Live Forever Club. I didn't want you to get stood up."

Aunt Winnie nods, beaming at the subterfuge. "That's right. Now you kids go out and enjoy your evening. If I have more fun than you, then you're doing it wrong." Aunt Winnie sidles up beside me and takes the rose. "I'll put this in a vase for you." She leans up to kiss my cheek. "I love you, honey cake. Go out and be irresponsible."

I hug her because I can't not. With life advice like that, it's no wonder that my aunt is one of my favorite people on the planet.

14

TWO CACTI

*D*o I know how to walk while holding a bucket of popcorn? Why yes, I do. Do I know how to drink sweet tea without spilling droplets onto my dress? Why yes, I do.

Of course, all of those things are easy if Logan isn't nearby.

"Let me hold those," he offers, taking the popcorn from me so I don't keep tripping over my own two feet, sending kernels cascading to the floor on the way from the concessions line to the theater.

"Thanks. I'm usually not this... Well, you know." I mean to explain my inelegance, but apparently simple sentences have deserted me right along with grace.

Logan offers his elbow to steady me, which of course, only makes me more unsteady. But still, I take it, marveling at what it feels like to be on the arm of a man who is the definition of breathtaking.

"Can I tell you a secret?" Logan asks me while Marianne and Carlos are chattering like two squirrels together behind us.

"Sure."

"I showed up at your house with my shirt on backwards. Winifred had to tell me, and I switched it before you came down. So if you're worried that you're the only one battling a few nerves, rest assured; we're both in that sinking ship together."

I cannot imagine Logan doing anything imperfect. I marvel up at him, my fingers lightly squeezing his bicep to connect us further. "Welcome aboard."

Logan and I walk to a row of seats halfway up the theater, deeming that as the best place to not be bothered by anyone else coming to see the same show. I haven't seen a thriller from this decade in a while. Whenever Winifred and I watch one of her movies that's on the intense side, it's been in black and white. This is going to be surround sound, full color and with the added tension of having Logan beside me.

Carlos and Marianne are in their own little world, talking animatedly. I wish I could observe them for hours without seeming rude. Marianne is even talking with her hands, not needing sentence after sentence pulled out of her. She is enamored of Carlos' clean-cut appearance, erect posture and smile that is directed solely at her.

Logan and I are mute by comparison.

We are five minutes early, so I resolve myself not to chicken out now. I'm already out of the house and on the date. The hardest part is over. Now I just have to be myself, which should be an easy thing for me to do.

I refuse to be a lousy date.

I gnaw on my lower lip, inhaling to steady myself while I get situated in my seat. "Winifred's got a garden in the backyard. It's so pretty. She was weeding it while I mowed the lawn today."

"I've learned there isn't much Winifred can't do."

His approval of my aunt's moxie endears me to him all the more. "I have a classically black thumb. I kill anything I try to grow. However, I think I should try again. New address, new me, right? Maybe I'm not bad at growing things anymore. Maybe all

I need is some Sweetwater Falls sunshine, and I'll be a natural at gardening."

The corner of Logan's mouth lifts. "I like that logic. How can we make this happen? Are you thinking of your own vegetable garden or some flowers?"

I grimace at his grand imagination. "I was thinking of a cactus. Those are pretty resilient, right?"

Logan snickers. "That sounds like a solid plan. We can build up some positive momentum with the cactus, and then shoot for something bigger."

"We?" I ask him, confused at his phrasing.

Logan offers me the popcorn once it's clear I'm a bit more relaxed, and therefore less likely to drop the snacks all over him. "I don't want to brag, but I also kill just about every plant my parents convince me passes for a fantastic birthday gift. Perhaps this is a hurdle I should figure out. We'll get better at this together."

"I love it. Can we start small, though? Just a cactus. I mean it. I don't want something crazy that I'll feel guilty for killing."

"There's a twenty-four-hour superstore in the next town over. They have a garden section. After the movie, I vote we ditch those lovebirds and go buy ourselves matching cacti."

I'm not sure I will ever stop smiling at this point. "Let's do it." I turn in my seat toward him, overjoyed that we had a fun exchange without the help of Marianne, and I didn't spill a single thing. "You know what else I always wondered about?"

His eyebrows dance with pure happiness. "Tell me."

"Who tends the flower boxes outside all of those businesses?"

Logan's nose scrunches. "I think each business takes care of their own."

"Huh. They all look so nice. I didn't realize everyone in Sweetwater Falls was so talented at growing things."

"Present company excepted."

The previews start, so Logan and I face the front, munching on popcorn with decidedly less anxiety than we walked in sporting. When Logan leans toward me, I instinctively lean closer. "Frank owns Nosy Newsy—the newsstand on Pear Street. I play poker with him once a month. He's got one of those flower boxes out front at his stand, too. The kind you see all over town. He's the only one who tends his flower box. I'm guessing if someone left you a flirty little note in there tomorrow behind the daisies and purple flowers, you would be the only person who would know about it, other than Frank, who is quite the secret keeper. He's never told anyone how terrible I am at poker."

I duck my head so my idiotic grin doesn't tip him off to the fact that I'm not all that adept at things like this. "Funny thing. I was planning on taking a walk by his store on Sunday. I might even stop by just to sniff the flowers."

Logan reaches for the popcorn at the same time I do, but he doesn't pull back his hand. Instead he flits his fingers over mine, holding my gaze in a manner that steals my breath away. "Then I'll do my best to write something clever. Make it worth the walk."

"Doggone," I accidentally say aloud.

Logan flinches. "Too much?"

"No. I was just hoping you might have a terrible personality. As it stands, I'm fairly certain I will never get over my crush on you if you keep this up."

Logan beams at me, then takes my hand and brings it to his lips. "I'm counting on exactly that, Miss Charlotte." He gives my knuckles a quick peck, sending heat flaring to my cheeks. Then he makes a bold move and keeps my hand, twining his fingers through mine as if that's how they were always meant to be.

His hand is sweaty.

When that small tidbit registers, relief sweeps over me. He's not faking insecurity to make me feel better about my own. He really is nervous.

I settle more comfortably in my seat, noting the swelling of my confidence as the room darkens.

Perhaps this could be viewed as a mild date for some, but for me it is a daring step forward. It's a mark of significance that not only can I make it through a date with my own personal celebrity, but I can also participate in semi-witty banter, complete with handholding.

When the movie begins, gratitude fills my chest. After all the stops and starts that met me on the way to this moment, perhaps I've landed someplace solid.

15

EVIDENCE AND INTUITION

When the movie ends, the four of us decide to go for a walk. Even though it's past twilight, there are enough streetlamps on to illuminate our path. I haven't had a clumsy moment in two hours. I'm high on my victory, however fleeting.

It helps that Logan offers his elbow to me, and I have nothing in my hands with which to juggle. Still, I count the whole thing as a win.

One thing I am learning about Logan is that he likes me in his space. I've hardly moved more than a foot from his side since the movie began, but he doesn't seem tired of me.

Marianne and Carlos whispered to each other through the first half of the movie before the actors proved interesting enough to quiet them down. Now that the credits are finished and there's no one to shush them, Marianne and Carlos are back into their rhythm.

I love watching Marianne without her veil of introversion. I don't know what it is about Carlos that disarms her quietude and brings out the best and bubbliest parts of her personality, but I am grateful he's here.

"I can't imagine that." Marianne remarks, shaking her head at Carlos. "Charlotte, Carlos bought his car without driving it first."

I chuckle at the two of them. "Well, that's the opposite of you, my dearest." Then to Carlos, I explain, "When Marianne bought her car, she had pages and pages of research. She test drove four of the same model but in different colors to see which gave her the right feel."

Carlos casts her a wry smile. "Why would the color of the car make it drive different?"

Marianne raises her nose in the air. "Well, I wanted to be sure. To not drive the car at all before you buy it? I cannot fathom that."

Carlos shrugs. "It's a lease. If I don't like it, I get rid of it in two years. Plus, how badly can they mess up a sedan? It's not like I have kids or specific needs for my car. Just get me from here to there. Drive me to Sweetwater Falls when I need good conversation that just has to be enjoyed in person."

Marianne burrows her forehead into his shoulder. They've migrated to handholding, which is just about the cutest thing in the world. His skin is a couple shades darker than Marianne's olive hue. They are totally precious together.

I decide to stick up for Carlos. "It's not wholly unheard of to buy something big without touching it first. That's what Ivan did, investing in Jared's business without seeing the building his money bought."

Marianne looks up at the stars in wonder. "And look at how well that turned out. Ivan was scammed out of thousands of dollars."

Carlos' steps slow. "Who's Ivan and what happened to him?"

Marianne fills in the blanks, though it seems Carlos is aware of much of the story thus far. "After Jared died, we made friends with Lisa Swanson, who everyone has thought for years was having an affair with him, but it turns out she and her husband were investing in Jared's startup. When he died, they were out ten thousand dollars. They thought they were the only investors, but it turns out Jared was hitting up several of his personal training clients to invest in the elite gym he was going to open. He asked them for money over and over, because the initial investment wasn't enough."

When she hands the story over to me, I don't hesitate. I'm just keyed up enough to bring Logan and Carlos into the scandal in hopes either of them might have any idea of how to help Lisa and Ivan. "I talked with Ivan this morning, actually. He got upset when Jared asked him for more money. Pushed him around a bit until Jared told him he had a building secured; he only needed more money to furnish the place and then the business could open. Ivan gave me the address, but when I got there, it was a tiny fast-food restaurant. Not for sale and not nearly enough space to be converted into a gym."

Logan and Carlos stop walking. "Are you serious?" Carlos asks, his face somber. "How many investors were there?"

I think back to my earlier conversation with the weightlifter. "Ivan knows of six people, all gone in for five grand apiece, plus whatever extra Jared was able to weasel out of them. Lisa invested the initial ten grand, plus an extra thousand dollars." I grimace that I spoke without thinking. "The extra grand was meant to be a secret. Her husband doesn't know about that. Sorry."

Logan's face is filled with concern. "We checked their accounts for the investigation. There was the ten grand they invested, but that's it. There's nothing extra that came out."

"Is that important?"

Logan rubs the nape of his neck. "It might be. I don't know. If she has money stashed away, there are quite a few things one could spend it on. They could invest in a business, or they could pay someone to make their problems go away." At my gasp, Logan shakes his head. "I'm sure it's nothing like that, but the fact that she didn't include that in the report is troubling. I need to call it in."

I hang my head in shame. "She told me that in confidence. I shouldn't have said it aloud. I wasn't thinking."

Logan moves his arm to wrap it around me while he makes a call with his free hand. He speaks to his father in short sentences, further tightening the knot in my chest. When he ends the call, Carlos is no less concerned. "Does Lisa have representation?"

Marianne's mouth pulls to the side. "For what? She's not under arrest. They haven't found evidence to link her to Jared's murder. I really don't think she did it, Carlos."

Logan corrects her, though not unkindly. "We don't have *enough* evidence. But there is plenty pointing us in her direction. This is one more piece. I don't want to upset you two, but you might have to start considering that the clues point a certain way for a reason."

I should be indignant and yank myself away from Logan for insinuating that Lisa might be anything shy of blameless. But instead, I cuddle closer, letting him draw my head to his shoulder in a one-armed embrace.

If I'm being honest with myself, there have been quite a few times I've muscled through that same logic, wondering if this sweet woman in my life might have a devious side that has yet to come to light. "I want her to be innocent. I truly believe she had nothing to do with this," I tell him, speaking into his chest.

Logan kisses the top of my head. "I know you do. I hope that, too."

Carlos gives our moment a minute to settle before he speaks up. "I wasn't asking if she had representation for a trial. I was asking if these people had anyone trying to get their money back."

Marianne and I turn our chins toward Carlos. "Is that even possible?" Marianne asks him.

Carlos holds his hand out and teeters it from side to side. "*Possible* is the right word. *Probable* is the wrong one. It's a long shot, but if they want even a portion of their money back, they'll need someone who knows the system and can file the appropriate motions to see if there are funds left to recover." He runs his thumb over Marianne's. "Is that something they might want? I don't want to insert myself when maybe what's best is to grieve and move on. And honestly, I'm swamped with work as it is." He motions to Marianne's face. "But whenever you get that worried look about you, my schedule suddenly clears and I fall all over myself volunteering for whatever it is that might erase that wrinkle between your eyebrows."

Marianne bumps her forehead to his shoulder. "From talking to Lisa, it sounds like she's equally upset about the death as she is the loss of that much money. Can't exactly blame her for being sore she got scammed." She frowns over at Logan. "It doesn't mean she's the killer."

Logan indulges in a long inhale. "No, but she's the one who purchased the peanut oil. And Jared is allergic to peanuts. Once I get word back on whether or not that was a factor in his death, I can form more of an opinion."

I speak up, though my voice sounds small. "But I don't want Lisa to be guilty."

Logan cups the back of my head, as if he's always known which small touches might calm my frustrations. "I'll make sure to add that to the list of evidence."

My lips purse. "I'm only going to try harder to prove Lisa is innocent, you know."

"I look forward to it. I'm sure she'll be off our list of suspects before the week is up, if you have anything to do with it. That's the thing about evidence. It doesn't have feelings and it can't lie."

I squint up at him. "Stop being good at your job and just take my side already."

The corner of Logan's mouth lifts. "How silly of me. Do you want me to take this side?" He pauses and lightly squeezes the left side of my waist, coaxing out a giggle and a squirm from me. Then he looks toward our friends. "Actually, Miss Charlotte and I have an errand to run before we call it a night. You two enjoy the moonlight."

When Logan's hand falls into mine, a giddy pep in my step emerges. I wish I could dismiss my suspicions that Lisa might actually be capable of murder, but my stubborn gut tells me my inclination to trust her is worth following.

If Logan needs evidence to prove her innocence, then I know that's exactly what I will need to find.

YOGA AND EVIDENCE

*W*hen Lisa invites me over to hang out on Sunday afternoon, I go with my best game face on. I am certain she is innocent, and I'm setting out to prove that to the world today. Surely I'll find some tidbit that pins her location far from Jared's. I'm here for sweet tea and her vegan gluten-free brownies, but really, I'm here on a mission to exonerate her.

Lisa is in workout clothes when she opens the door of the one-story abode. I love the elegant hunter green shutters against the red brick of her home. "Yay! I can't tell you the last time I had a friend over my house just for fun." She waves for me to come inside.

I love that we hug each other just to say hello.

Innocent. Innocent, my gut chimes.

Prove it, my head replies.

Everything is immaculate. Not just clean, but pristine and polished. I take my shoes off, wondering if I should apologize to the welcome mat for stepping on it.

"Honey, Lisa is here. Come say hello." Then to me, Lisa says, "He's been working a lot, what with the library roof needing repair, but he wanted to meet you. He just got home and hopped in the shower."

When Welsey rounds the corner, his hair is wet and he's tucking in his blue button-down. "I was hoping to catch you before I had to head back out. Good to meet you. You're the new girl, right? Lisa's friend from the big city."

That's a nice change. Usually I'm the new girl, Winifred's niece—a badge I wear proudly. But look at me, making friends so easily.

I beam at him. "That's exactly who I am. Charlotte McKay."

"Wesley. I gotta say, my wife has been so happy since you came into our lives. Good timing, I guess."

Gosh, he's sweet. What a nice guy. He's shorter than both Lisa and myself, and carries himself with a peppy smile that filters through his entire body.

Of course Lisa wouldn't cheat on this guy. Why would people assume that?

"Lisa's been a godsend. I wouldn't have opened up my cupcake business if she hadn't pushed me to really try."

Wesley's hand flits to Lisa's back. "That's my Lisa. Always got that business hat on." A shadow flickers over his eyes. "You're the best kind of business owner—looking for guidance, not a handout."

I grimace. I mean, it's not like I paid Lisa for her business prowess. Maybe I should have offered. "I'm so grateful for her advice." And I truly am.

Lisa elbows her husband good naturedly. "I know you've got to get going. It's girl time, so scram. No boys allowed."

"That's my cue."

Lisa moves to the dining room table. "Are you going to the grocery store, Wesley? Because you got peanut oil last time. I need coconut oil for the sugar scrubs I'm making. Can you return the peanut oil?"

Wesley shakes his head. "I threw away the receipt, babe. Sorry."

"I know. I picked it out of the garbage because the oil needs to be returned." She picks up her purse and fishes through the contents, frowning. "I thought I nabbed the receipt and put it in here, but I can't seem to find it."

At mention of the possible key ingredient in the recipe of Jared's murder, my hearing sharpens, and my brain clicks into overdrive. I'm not sure I have a believable poker face. I do my best to concoct one so I don't give away that peanut oil might be the murder weapon.

The hairs on the nape of my neck stand on end.

Wesley moves to the front door and slides on his loafers. "I'll pick up the coconut oil for you. We can return the other stuff another day when you find the receipt."

"You're the best. Meeting a potential client for a bid?" she inquires.

"Sure am."

"Good luck, babe." She migrates to his side and gives him a quick peck before he exits.

I make my most excellent effort to school my features. After all, I don't know for sure that peanut oil is the murder weapon. He could have just been forgetful and bought the wrong kind. There is such a wide variety of oil out there.

My steps are careful as we walk into the kitchen and sit at their pristine breakfast nook. The kitchen is all white and blue with a French country theme. I feel as if I'm smack in the middle of a modern country catalog, complete with white teacups and saucers with blue rims.

"As promised," she says, motioning to the living room where two yoga mats are set out. "I'll do a class for Marianne when she comes over someday. But today, it's you and me."

My eyes widen, not expecting a yoga tutorial. "I'm not sure

I'll be any good at this." I motion to my khaki shorts and yellow blouse. "Is this okay to wear? Don't I need fancy workout clothes?"

"It's perfect." She chuckles at my worry. "You look as if I've just told you we'll be eating spiders for lunch. It's not all that complicated. In fact, yoga tends to *un*complicate a whole lot of things for me. Maybe it will have the same effect on you."

I swallow hard, trying to force the alarms going off in my head about the peanut oil to silence themselves. "Let's do it, then. I could use some Zen." I force a smile. "See? I even know the words. Zen. That's a yoga thing, right?"

Lisa smirks at me. "Let's start with a long stretch and see how far we get."

Over the next half an hour, Lisa leads me in a Mountain Pose, Downward-Facing Dog, Crescent Lunge, the Warrior II, the Triangle, and the Plank Pose. My limbs feel as if they are lengthening while simultaneously strengthening as the minutes tick by.

I tapped out shortly after the Plank Pose. I worry she can spot my suspicion and found a way to punish me with impossible to hold poses.

When the session ends, my limbs are rubbery. "Am I taller? I feel taller." I stretch my torso, wondering if I stand at a commanding five-foot-eleven-inches now.

"The tallest," Lisa agrees, not looking nearly as winded as I am. She fixes two cups of tea for us so we can settle in at the kitchen table.

I would have thought the yoga would grant me tranquility, but even after all that stretching, my heart is racing. When Lisa brings the mugs to the table, I still haven't found a way to brush off the fact that it was Wesley who bought the peanut oil, and not Lisa.

"So, tell me everything. Texting isn't the same. How are you on making back your initial startup investment in the Bravery Bakery?" Lisa's face is painted with glee because business plans and startups are what make her come alive. I can't believe she doesn't do this for a living. She's so passionate about it. She has a knack for making momentum out of a mess.

I swallow the kneejerk reaction that always undersells my happiness if it sounds the least bit like it might be bragging. Lisa is my friend; she's not going to judge me or be put off because of my happiness. "Actually, we're in the black. The first week's sales covered the business cards, filing fee and ingredients, website hosting, no problem. From here on out, it's pure profit."

Lisa squeals, making her seem far younger than her fifty years. "Oh, I'm so happy! I knew you were a solid candidate to become a business owner. And all without more than word of mouth advertising? That means you've got a hot product."

I love her enthusiasm. I'm just as passionate about cupcakes, so our fervors feed off each other nicely.

Lisa has a pad of paper and pen all ready for us. I had a feeling that a girl day with yoga, tea and gluten-free brownies might turn into business building time. Gotta love a girl with passion in her soul and organization on her side.

"Maybe it's a novelty thing. I wonder if the wave of orders is going to crest and die out after the first few weeks." Hedging my bets with success keeps me from hoping too hard that this could actually be the thing I end up doing in life.

Lisa tsks me. "We can't go thinking small like that. People are buying your cupcakes because they are amazing. The business model is sustainable because *I* am amazing." Then she scribbles on her notepad. "But yes, we need to build an advertising plan to make sure this success isn't a one-time wave, but a tsunami that only keeps growing."

I laugh airily through my nose when I picture a tidal wave of cupcakes flooding the town of Sweetwater Falls. "I like that.

Honestly, there are so many orders, I'm not sure I can keep up if there were to be more. I have a day job, and Bill isn't exactly the understanding type if I want to call in to bake all day from home."

Lisa grins at me. "That, my friend, is a very good problem to have. Let's set a dollar amount, then. A certain number you'll need in your business bank account and a certain number you'll need in your personal account in order to quit working at the diner."

My eyes widen. "What? That's not possible. There's no way I could quit. I have to have some money coming in."

Lisa taps her temple. "I know that. That's why you're not going into the diner right now and quitting. All in good time."

"I didn't even know that was a possibility," I admit to her, peering at her notes.

She tears off a second sheet for me. "Okay, write down the number you need to have in the bank (both personal and business) in order to be able to quit. Then write down what you make at the diner. You'll want two full months of that income from cupcakes to be able to quit. Those two factors are quite important."

I massage my temples. "How did you learn all of this?"

"The School of Hard Knocks," Lisa jokes. "Just kidding. Business school. Plus, I help Wesley when he needs it. I used to consult before I got married."

"I had no idea, but it makes perfect sense. You're thinking of everything."

"Not quite. Now you're going to make a list of supplies you'll need to have already bought before you can quit." She twirls her hand in the air, coming up with a list on the spot. "Extra cupcake pans, oven mitts, expensive ingredients you have budget for to purchase. I dunno. I'm not all that familiar with your specific needs, but you are."

In truth, I have a few things I could stand to upgrade. "I could use more of those twenty-four cupcake pans. But those aren't super expensive. I just haven't gotten around to buying them."

"Time is money," Lisa sings, writing that down on the list.

I rattle off a few other things that I don't need with any sort of urgency, but if this actually becomes a thing, those purchases will set me up for an easier life.

The secondary reason I came over today is still a niggling thought at the back of my mind as I write. I tap the butt of the pen against my cheek while I think. "I need to be super specific about what goes on this list. I don't want to accidentally put down something vague and then buy the wrong thing." I conjure up a smirk for her. "Like going to the store for coconut oil and coming back with peanut oil."

We share a snicker.

Lisa rolls her eyes good naturedly at her husband's mistake. "Honestly, I don't know how anyone could get those things confused. I don't even know what to do with peanut oil."

"Have you tried any recipes yet?"

Lisa shakes her head. "I'm not what you would call an adventurous cook."

I stand. "Point me to your pantry. There might be a recipe on the bottle."

I meander in the direction Lisa aims me. My breath quickens because I am praying I don't come face to face with the murder weapon.

I poke around in her pantry while Lisa looks over my list of things to purchase for my business. She scribbles a few more items, for which I am grateful. However, it makes me worry that I have no idea what I'm doing. Why would I think I can open a business? I can't even keep a plant alive.

No. I'm changing that narrative. Logan and I stayed out until two in the morning after the movie ended Friday night. We went to the twenty-four-hour superstore located in the next town over, which features a more bustling and city-like semi-metropolis than the cute town of Sweetwater Falls. We giggled and talked animatedly while we selected two matching cacti. Then we walked around the store just to have more time together.

It was the perfect date.

My chin lifts with renewed determination as my eyes scan Lisa's organized shelves. If I can keep that cactus alive, then I can open a business.

I'm not sure there's a direct correlation, but that's what I tell myself.

When my gaze snags on the peanut oil, my stomach drops. "Lisa? You said you didn't use the peanut oil. Did you open it?"

Lisa laughs. "What for? You're a good sport for trying to find a recipe, though."

The eight-ounce bottle has most definitely been opened. An inch of the viscous liquid is missing.

"Lisa?" my voice cracks. "Would you mind if I borrowed your peanut oil? Maybe I can figure out a decent cupcake to make with it."

Lisa waves off my weird request. "Take it. Goodness knows I don't know what to do with it. And that receipt is long gone. I need to start keeping better track of the thousands of slips of paper that float in and out of our lives."

I swallow hard and cast around for a grocery bag, so as not to get my fingerprints on the bottle. Though, Wesley bought it. Even if by some stretch of reason Wesley is innocent, his fingerprints would still be on the bottle.

I would make a terrible detective.

"Huh," I say, turning to Lisa. "Maybe Wesley got creative after all. The bottle is opened and a bit of it is gone."

Lisa's nose scrunches. "Weird. He hasn't used it for anything he's cooked me so far. Maybe he'll surprise me with something new for dinner tonight." She taps the list. "I think this is good. It's actually not all that much. I don't know how expensive all of this will be, but my best guess makes me think you'll be able to buy all of this within the month."

"Unless you added a diamond necklace to the list, I can buy all of that stuff next week, using only profits from the bakery."

Lisa whistles. "You just might get your dream sooner than you think."

My heart should be soaring, and part of it probably is. But the other half of me is devastated that I may have found the murder weapon. Either my new friend is the killer, or I'll devastate her world if it comes out that it's her husband at fault.

I smile my way through two of her gluten-free dairy-free brownies, even though they taste like raisins and paste.

When I fold the list and put it in my pocket two hours later as I go to leave, I whirl around and hug Lisa tight before I exit. "Thank you. No matter how it all turns out, just know that I'm so grateful I met you."

Lisa softens and drags her hand up and down my spine. "Aw, me too, Charlotte. Like the little sister I never knew I needed."

My heart sinks because I feel the same way about her—like I don't mind her bossing me around as an older sister would.

When I slide my key into the ignition, I know I won't be headed home to test out new cupcake recipes.

I don't want to be the one to bring this to the police, but I know if there's any justice to be had for Jared, that's exactly what I have to do.

SUBMITTING A STATEMENT

The sun is low in the sky when I arrive at the police station. I've gnawed on my lower lip the entire way, so much that I'm surprised I don't taste blood when I turn off the engine. I need to go inside and report what I've learned, but no part of me wants to. From where I sit, if Jared died of a peanut allergy, then the two most likely culprits are either Wesley or Lisa. And being that Lisa thought the bottle of peanut oil was still sealed, I'm fairly certain Wesley is the one who opened it. Unless he all of a sudden decided to get crazy in the kitchen, the evidence most likely points the accusatory finger his way.

I lean my forehead on the steering wheel, closing my eyes so I can hope against hope that I am wrong. I don't want to accuse an innocent Lisa at best or take away her husband and ruin her marriage at worst.

If people didn't talk about her before, they certainly will now.

When knuckles rap against my window, I startle, sitting upright.

A wave of happy nerves that feels strikingly similar to

nausea trills up and down my midsection. "Logan?" I roll down the window. "What are you doing here?"

He shoots me a wry smile. "I work here. How about you? Good day to sit in the police parking lot with your existential dread, eh?"

I must have that look about me. "I don't know what to do," I admit, my shoulders lowering.

Logan tilts his head to the side. "I've got a few minutes before I have to be in there. Want to talk about it?"

I motion for him to get in the car, unwilling to have this awful conversation out in the open. I'm grateful there is only my purse and the bag with the peanut oil in the passenger seat, so I don't have to apologize for the mess as I clear the space for him to sit. After our date, I still feel nervous and ungraceful around him, but my lips have unlocked, which allows me to be myself finally, thank goodness.

"What's going on, Miss Charlotte?" Though there isn't a flirty tease in his tone, I still have to fight against the flush that feathers across my cheeks.

"I'm here to talk to your father," I admit.

Logan's eyebrows dance. "About your intentions? He already knows we're dating." I can tell he's in a good mood. Though, what his foul mood might look like, I have no idea.

"Dating, are we? Will there be another date?"

Logan reaches across the console and brushes his fingers across mine. "After you tell me what's on your mind, I say we make setting the next date a top priority."

My chin dips as my mind does a happy dance. It's hard to tamp down the merriment, but I do my best. I didn't come here to flirt (though that is a happy surprise). "I'm here because I don't know what to do. I should be in there, talking to your dad about what I found, but my feet won't seem to get me inside."

Logan's mouth pulls to the side. "Funny thing, feet. They

need a good reason to get you places. What do you want to talk to him about?"

My voice lowers as my hands grip the steering wheel. "I may have found the murder weapon in Jared's case."

Logan sobers. "That seems like a good enough reason to go inside."

"Is it?" My face is filled with that one question above all else. "I like Lisa. Sweetwater Falls didn't give her a fair chance, like it did me. Everyone thinks she was cheating on Wesley all these years, but she wasn't."

"So Lisa is the killer? Tell me how you landed there—not that I disagree."

"She helped me, Logan. She's still helping me. Without Lisa, I wouldn't have taken this leap and started the Bravery Bakery from home. She took a chance on me. She invested her time and patience, building a plan to help me make this a success. She jumped in right on the heels of her helping someone else build a business, and it blew up in her face."

Logan doesn't speak to fill the silence when I run out of steam, but gives me the space to build up more, so I can vent everything without interruption.

"She loves Wesley, and he adores her. If I go into that police station and tell them what I found, it could sink their perfectly happy marriage. And it's not as if she's got a good support system to get her through this. People talk *about* her, not *to* her. It's the one dismal thing about this incredible town."

Again, Logan nods but doesn't say anything.

More upset that's been burbling inside of me spills out. "And Jared, from what I've learned, was a bad guy. He scammed people out of thousands upon thousands of dollars. And I'm going to sink a perfectly happy marriage because of that?" I hold up my hands as if Logan has argued with me. "Death isn't the appropriate punishment for theft, but it's not as if Jared was the type to go around walking old ladies across the street. He stole from people—habitually, might I add. Stole and lied and then did it again and again to more people. I don't blame him for attacking Jared."

Logan finally speaks. "Him? I thought we were building to Lisa being the culprit."

I lower my head. "I was at their house today, determined to find something to prove Lisa didn't do it."

"And what did you find?"

"Remember the receipt from the store that proves they didn't stay home during Jared's time of death? It had peanut oil and gum on it."

"And Jared is allergic to peanut oil, which Lisa knew."

I shake my head. "Lisa didn't buy the peanut oil, Logan. Wesley bought it. Lisa had put coconut oil on the grocery list, so he went to the store in the next town over to buy not coconut oil but peanut oil 'by mistake.' Lisa laughed it off, thinking nothing of it. Said she didn't even know what to do with peanut oil because she doesn't cook much. Said she hadn't opened the bottle yet because she was hoping to return it." I blink at Logan. "But she can't because she lost the receipt."

"The receipt she built your plan on and gave to you."

"Exactly."

Logan's brows push together. "But what does that prove? There's no way to know if she's telling the truth."

I reach into the backseat where I stashed the peanut oil and grab the bag, bringing it into view. "Logan, when I went into the pantry, the bottle was opened. Look how much is missing. I'd say that's enough to trigger a reaction if someone is allergic, wouldn't you?"

"But that doesn't..."

"Lisa didn't open it, Logan. I'm almost positive that Wesley did. He's the one who went to the store to buy it. He's most likely the person who opened the bottle."

"They both said they stayed home all evening, though."

"Wouldn't you lie to help your husband avoid suspicion? Especially if he went out to run an errand for you."

Logan swallows hard. "How did you come to possess this? Did you steal it?"

I shake my head. "I asked her if I could take it home to experiment with cupcake recipes."

"Good, Charlotte. Then it's admissible as legitimate evidence. Did you pour any out to smell or taste it?"

"I didn't even open the thing. I came straight from her house. I thought the sheriff should decide whether or not this is a smoking gun."

Logan turns in his seat to more fully face me. "Why didn't you call me? This is kind of my entire job. If I had a baking question, I wouldn't think to call up Winifred. I'd go straight to you."

My neck shrinks. "You know why."

Logan casts around as if he cannot imagine a reason on earth that would keep me from calling him about something this important. "I really don't."

I motion to his face and his entire being. "Because you're handsome. Sometimes I have a hard time getting through simple sentences if you're around."

Logan spreads his hands out. "But we just talked through the entire thing in here."

My mouth falls open, surprised at the evidence he's presenting me. "We did. Maybe I'm getting over my crush. Finally, I don't have to be so nervous around you."

Logan backpedals. "Wait a second. Of course I don't want you to be nervous around me. I'm hardly an intimidating presence. But you don't have a crush on me anymore? What part of our date turned you off?"

I laugh airily, covering my mouth. "I only mean that I can finally be a person around you without tripping over my own two feet." I take a chance with my bravery and reach across the divide so I can pat his cheek in the most patronizing way one can do such a thing. "You're still very pretty, Logan."

He grumbles good naturedly under his breath, but then refocuses on the matter at hand. "It was good of you to come in to report this. We're supposed to get the results in from the coroner today to see if there was an allergic reaction factoring into the cause of death. If not, then your crisis of conscience can melt away. The peanut oil might have nothing to do with Jared's death."

"Wouldn't that be great?" Sunshine begins to filter through my dismal disposition. "What if there was no allergic reaction at all? What if Wesley just happened to buy an already opened container from the store without noticing? I mean, he was supposed to pick up coconut oil for Lisa, so he wasn't exactly paying attention. Stranger things have happened, right?"

"I'm sure they have."

"Maybe you'll get the call today that Jared was strangled to death, and that's that. Lisa and Wesley are free and clear."

"Well, I mean, there still is a dead body on our hands. So there's that. We'll be back at square one, but that's nowhere we haven't been before."

My spine lengthens as my whole being perks up. "That would be so wonderful. Then you'll find whoever did it— whoever was angry enough about losing out on money to strangle Jared to death—and Lisa can be cleared of all suspicion."

"Sounds like there was quite a list of people angry enough to murder."

"None of them would..." But I stop myself from finishing that thought. "Ivan pushed Jared around a bit. Physical intimidation and whatnot. I'm not sure how bad it got, but yeah. I guess you're right about the list of suspects being far more than just Wesley and Lisa."

Logan takes the bottle from me and then twines his fingers through mine. "One step at a time. I'll log this all in, since I just took your statement. You go about your normal day, okay? We don't know how Jared died, so for now do me the simple favor of staying away from the Swansons." When I make to protest, he holds up his hand in surrender. "Just until we have more information. So things like going over their house and being alone with either of them—that's the kind of thing I'm hoping you won't do until all of this is settled."

"Oh, fine. But it's not Lisa. I'll bet it's one of the other investors. Not Ivan, of course, but one of the others."

"I'm sure you're right. But until then..."

I exhale and lean back in my seat. "I won't be alone with either of the Swansons until we've crossed them off our list of suspects."

"Thank you, Miss Charlotte." He brings my fingers to his lips so he can give them a quick kiss. "In case you're wondering if seeing you is the best start of my workday, it truly is."

A blush too potent to stifle takes over my cheeks.

Logan smirks at the pink coloring face. "There it is. If I can make you blush, then I've still got a shot with you."

His phrasing sends my head spinning. Why would he think there is anyone on earth he would not have a shot at dating? And how could he possibly think I would ever turn him down?

"Next Friday night, I would love to take you out—without Marianne and Carlos. Might that be possible?"

A shocking thought crosses my mind: I wonder what it would be like to kiss Logan. My tongue sweeps over my lower lip before I can rein in my reaction to his obvious appeal. "I would love that. Yes."

Logan is nothing if not adorable when he smiles at me, squeezing my hand before he opens his door to exit. "Looking forward to it. If you're going home, can you tell Winifred I know it's her who's responsible for my dad's bad mood this week? Also tell her I can be bribed into silence with lemonade and fresh tomatoes from her garden."

I raise my chin. "I know nothing about any toilet papering of any home ever. Winifred is a saint of a woman. An ideal citizen."

Logan chuckles, kissing my fingers once more before he slips out of my car. "Don't get into too much trouble, Miss Charlotte."

"I'm going to stack books at the library. Trouble is going to have to work real hard to find me in there."

He leans down to peek at me one last time. "Might want to stop by Nosy Newsy on your way. I hear the purple flowers are particularly chatty this morning."

Joy beams out of me at the prospect of getting a secret note from Logan, hidden in plain sight.

I watch Logan walk into the precinct, wondering how my life has opened up so much that I am now dating the handsomest, sweetest man in the universe.

If not for the murder, I would say that life couldn't possibly get any better than it is now.

18

CHECKING OUT

*M*arianne is the worst offender of breaking the "don't be loud in the library" rule, which always takes me aback, considering she is the head librarian. "Read it again. I need to parse it for subtext."

I love how into the small flirty moments she can be. "I'm not sure there's a subtext in Logan's letter. It's only two paragraphs long."

"Don't you know what you have here? Don't you know what this is? This is Jane Austen's *Persuasion*. This is the stuff great love stories are made of. You are living your own literary adventure." When I chuckle at her theatrics, she jabs her finger at the note. "Don't you dare treat this as if it's a grocery list. This is the beginning of an epic romance."

I shake my head, snickering at her enthusiasm. I pick up the next book and scan it in, smiling at the little beep the machine makes. "I'm the appropriate amount of gleeful about the whole thing. It all feels too perfect, like if I sneeze it might go away."

"I'll be careful not to sneeze on the note, then." Marianne picks up the paper once more, ignoring the stack of books that need to be sorted so she can pour over the letter again. She sighs contentedly, as if Logan's cute and quirky sentences are actually Shakespeare's missing epistles.

Gotta love her.

I smile and wave at Henry before he leaves with a book in his hand. He was the only patron in the library, and now it's just the two of us. It's just as well. The time is nearing six o'clock, which is when the library closes for the evening.

Henry holds the door open for Wesley, who trots in with a smile aimed at Marianne and me. "Hi, girls. Stopping by to take a look at my handiwork. The inspection is tomorrow." He flashes us a thumbs up, to which I grin.

I hope I'm grinning. Being in the same giant building as him makes me acutely aware of my current working theory that Wesley Swanson is, in fact, the killer.

He moves toward the back of the library, out of sight and out of earshot.

Marianne grimaces at me, pointing at my face. "What's that expression supposed to be?"

"It's a smile."

"Really? Because it looks like you're being choked." She slaps her hand over her mouth. "Sorry. Poor choice of words. I sure hope they catch whoever killed Jared."

I keep my voice low while I scan in the last of the books, creating a giant mountain for Marianne to sort and shelve. "I'm trying not to look like I suspect Wesley of murder. I just turned in what might possibly be evidence in the crime."

Marianne freezes. "Um, what?"

I take my time going over the details I shared with Logan this afternoon, laying out why exactly I am certain Wesley is the killer.

"But that's all supposing the peanut oil is the murder weapon. Why would there have been bruising on Jared's neck? Why would someone poison him *and* choke him to death?"

"Crime of passion mixed with premeditated murder?"

"I'm not sure that's a thing."

I shrug as I start in to help Marianne sort through the books. "I wish none of this was a thing. I wish Sweetwater Falls was a place with zero scandal and never-ending cupcakes."

Marianne giggles as she sets a few more books onto a pile. "I love that your version of utopia includes cupcakes."

When my buzzing phone interrupts us, I sigh. "It's Logan."

She points to my frown. "That's not the face of someone who just got a love note."

"It's not love related. He said he would call when they narrowed down cause of death." I hold the phone to my ear, worry weighting my features. "Hi, Logan."

"The next time I call you, it will have nothing to do with murder."

"Next time, sure. But this time, that's all I want to talk about. Did you hear from the coroner?"

"You were right," Logan says, his tone grave. "Jared didn't die from strangulation. He died of anaphylactic shock. He was choked either mid or postmortem."

"Why would anyone do that?"

"My guess is to throw us off the trail. Whoever did it would have to have known of Jared's peanut allergy. There are only two people in all of Sweetwater Falls who had that sort of information. And one of them bought peanut oil the day of Jared's murder."

Bile rises in my throat. "Wesley Swanson killed Jared," I whisper.

Marianne's eyes widen.

"There's a police detail on their way to his house now to bring him in."

"There's only one problem with that, Logan. Wesley is here now."

"Here, where?"

"At the library. I'm helping Marianne close down for the night. We'll stall him, but you need to get here now."

"Charlotte, be careful." Logan's concern tugs at my heart.

The moment I end the call, the lights go out, bathing us in darkness. My sharp inhale is the only thing I hear, but for the fluttering of pages from Marianne closing a book beside me.

Marianne groans. "I was afraid this might happen. With all the work being done updating the building, it was only a matter of time before something went wrong. I knew it was all coming together too smoothly."

But I am not convinced that the power outage is the fault of the construction. The contractor is in the building, but he's not making a sound. There is no shuffling of feet or calling out to make his presence known.

I grasp around in the dark for Marianne's wrist, bringing her down to crouch behind the desk. "I have a bad feeling about this," I whisper.

I can hear the frown in Marianne's reply. "The emergency lights should be coming on. That's why we have them."

"And I'm sure Wesley knows how to turn them off. He must have heard me talking to Logan. He knows that we know he is the killer!"

Realization dawns on Marianne. Her pulse quickens beneath my fingertips. "We need to call the police!" she whispers.

"I just did," I remind her. "Logan is on his way. We just have to wait it out."

But when the sound of loafers hitting the floor greets my ears, I know we might have run out of time.

19

QUICK AND QUIET

*T*he footsteps are slow and menacing through the library as they move toward us. "Wesley knows where we are. He must have overheard me telling Logan I know he is the killer," I whisper to Marianne. My eyes are adjusting to the darkness, allowing me to make out my best friend's silhouette. I'm not sure if that gives me more reassurance or less. I want to know when Wesley is coming, but on the other hand, he can now detect us if we try to escape. "We have to move."

I can hear the panic in Marianne's voice. "The front door is too far away! If we run, it's not like we'll be safe once we get outdoors. He'll follow us. There's no one there, and my car is parked at the back of the lot!"

"Mine too." It seemed a courtesy to the guests at the library for me to park far away and give them the good spots. Now I wish I had been selfish and taken the closest one. "We can't stay behind the desk. He's coming this way!"

Marianne grips my hand and inches her body closer to mine. "We can crawl toward the back exit. Quick!"

Quick and quiet are not the same thing. I'm not sure which is more important in this moment. Nerves peak as Marianne grips my wrist harder than I can withstand.

She leads the way on hands and knees while the footsteps near with sickening purpose. The floor is hard, bruising my knees as I scuttle after Marianne. Her whimpers are not silent, but I pray they don't reach Wesley's ears and give away our location.

I've never been in the back room for librarians only. I vaguely know which direction it lies but cannot recall if it's a push door or a handle to turn. Does the handle have a lock? Is there a way to get in without the door clicking open and shut? Does it need a key to get in, and if it does, does Marianne have it with her?

Haunting shapes of bookstacks manifest in my vision, but it is too dark to be sure of what the smaller rectangles and squares are. Can we hide behind anything to conceal our presence? Is there something that might be used as a weapon if the need should arise?

We can't crawl quickly without making rustling noises with our clothes, so it's a measured escape. I can't gage the distance from myself to my destination. When Wesley's voice fills the library, I know we aren't far enough away from him to give me any real assurance that we might get out of this unscathed.

"Charlotte McKay, I think we need to have a little conversation." Wesley's voice carries a singsong quality to it, making it seem like he wants to discuss fun town gossip. "I think you're under the impression that I've done something wrong. I need you to call the police and tell them you're mistaken. You didn't find what you thought you did. You dumped out some of the peanut oil yourself. That seems like a fair trade. My wife works to build you a plan for your business, and you do this one favor for us."

I gnaw on my lower lip, keeping any sounds of distress locked inside.

"Lisa has a good life now, thanks to Jared being gone. He was a criminal, Charlotte. He robbed us. All I did was make sure he couldn't hurt anyone ever again."

The urge to argue is strong, but I steel myself against engaging.

His voice is coming from the desk where we just were, which means he is far closer to us now than we can afford.

I crawl at Marianne's heels, so when she veers right and stops behind the first bookstack we come across, I follow suit. It's a far cry from the back exit, but there's no way we'll make it there without Wesley detecting our movements, however shrouded by shadow they might be. Our fingers entwine because if this is truly our last moment, we will face it together.

I can hear Wesley shuffling near the circulation desk, no doubt checking to see if we're hiding behind anything there. My heart pounds so loud; I worry even that might carry through the echoing walls of the library.

I cast around, looking for anything that might serve as a weapon in case it comes to that. All we have to do is wait out Logan's arrival. If we can stay hidden until then, we'll be okay.

The library is hauntingly beautiful, even in the dark. I lean against the bookstack, my back to Wesley as he rummages around the area we just left. The shadows lurk and linger, letting me know that we are not the only horrors who find shelter in these walls. There are murder mysteries, romance novels, biographies, cookbooks, reference books, children's books and any number of genres that have found a home here.

This is Marianne's happy place.

Determination solidifies in my stomach, sweeping away the fear that would paralyze me into inaction. Marianne will not die in her happy place. She may not believe she is Marianne the

Wild, but I *know* that I am Charlotte the Brave. I faced my fears and opened a bakery, declaring to Sweetwater Falls and the world that this is my dream, and it's worth fighting for.

I am worth fighting for.

These books have a home here, and right now, I need them to fight with me.

I turn around, facing the direction of the circulation desk. "Steady, Marianne," I whisper. "I need you to get ready. When he comes this way, we're going to push this giant shelf over. Then we'll run for the back exit."

"I can't!" Marianne frets. I can hear the panicked tears in her voice.

I grip her hand as she turns in like motion. "Yes, you can. You're the head librarian. These books need you to protect them from Wesley. They don't deserve to be afraid like this. He's about to bring violence into your happy place. Time to defend your turf, sweetheart."

Marianne sniffles and then throws her arms around my neck, squeezing a little too tight. "Okay. Yes. You're right. He's not going to kill me here. Not like this."

"Not ever."

Marianne reaches past me and touches something on the ground. "You have to pull the pin. The shelves are anchored to the floor." She turns her wrist and something metallic screeches too loud for my liking.

I cringe, but it's too late. Wesley's footsteps still.

"Hurry! The other one!" I whisper to her.

Marianne doesn't bother keeping her movements silent. Our location has already been given away.

I stand on quaking legs, my knees debating whether or not they will commit to holding me upright. I don't know if this will work, but it's our only option. We can't wait for Logan anymore. Plus, I don't know what sort of weapon Wesley might have on him. Peanut oil won't work to silence me but strangling sure will. I don't want Logan anywhere near that.

The pin being pulled from the far end isn't nearly as loud. When Marianne comes back to me, she presses her hands to the shelf, nodding once to let me know she has her wits about her. "We need to know where he's at so we know when to push."

I close my eyes and nod, swallowing hard. I don't want to give away our location any more than we already have, but this is the risk I know we have to take.

My hands grip the shelf. "Wesley, you can't do this," I call out. "You murdered someone, and now you want to silence me?"

I can practically picture Wesley's head jerking toward us. "You don't know what it's like to be cheated out of thirteen thousand dollars."

My nose scrunches. "I thought it was ten." Plus Lisa's extra thousand, but I don't mention that.

"I put in three grand without telling Lisa. Jared asked for more. Said it would help him secure a building. But then he gave me the address, and I found out it was nothing but a fast-food building—too small to house a real gym, like he promised."

Same thing that happened to Ivan, only it looks like Wesley did his homework. "Is that when you knew he was swindling you?"

"That's when I invited him to meet me at the fair after it closed for the night. I confronted him, but when he told me the money was gone, I lost it. I wasn't going to give him the lemonade with the peanut oil in it. I was going there to get our money back. Had he done the right thing, all of this could have been avoided." Wesley's voice is closer now, but not close enough.

"Why strangle him?"

Wesley chuckles, though I can't imagine anything less funny. "That was me being clever. I thought it would draw attention away from the peanut oil." A few more steps, and Wesley will be close enough for us to push this over onto him. "Jared deserved it, you know. My wife worked tirelessly on his business plan, and he did nothing with it. He bought himself a new car."

Marianne sniffles, her tears becoming audible.

I don't know if Wesley is close enough, because he's gone silent, along with his footsteps. But I know if we don't act now, it might be too late. I tap Marianne's wrist to the count of three, hoping she knows that when the third beat comes, we're going to push this thing over and run.

Though I am terrified, I know I can be brave. If it means saving Marianne from harm, I can do just about anything.

The bookstack is heavier than I anticipated, but I don't give up. I throw my entire body's weight against it, and Marianne does the same. For a second, I worry we didn't take out the right pins because nothing budges. This was the grand plan for our escape. There is no Plan B.

Wesley's voice is calm, laced with a cruelty that makes my spine tingle. He was so nice this morning when we shook hands in his home. "You know, you don't have to..."

But I don't get to hear the end of his sentence. Marianne and I push once more, and finally, it is enough. It's not just us fighting for our freedom anymore; the books come to our aid. Marianne spends her days respecting and adoring them. Now it's their turn to fight for us.

The shelf creaks, but that is the only alert Wesley has. He's too close to dart out of the way. The shelf stretches at least ten feet high, and when it tips over, it unleashes a triumphant cry into the darkness on our behalf.

Wesley howls, I'm not sure if it's from pain or surprise, but either way, this is our chance to escape.

Marianne grabs my wrist, shrieking because something has to announce her switch from meek to wild. I love both sides of her personality. Very few get to witness her reckless side. I count myself lucky to hold onto her hand while she leads the way to the back of the library. We keep each other upright as we side-step books, trip over a stool and smack into several things we can't make out in the dark.

Marianne collides with the door, fumbling with the handle. Her grip slips over and over when Wesley cries out in anger. I can't tell if he's on his feet and coming for us, and I don't want to find out.

Marianne finally gets the door open, leading me inside a room I've never seen before. I have no sense of direction. There aren't any stained-glass windows in here to let in the barest amount of light for me to make out vague shapes. I trip over a chair while Marianne cries without holding back her volume. I don't know where the back exit is, but I follow her, making sure not to let go of her hand. My heart pounds almost as loud as her incoherent sobs.

We feel around in the dark when we run smack into a wall. "I can't find the exit!" she cries. "He cut the emergency lights! Where is the door?"

When my hand flits to what I hope is a door's handle, I yank on it. Now it's my own sobs I hear as we run out into the twilight. I'm aiming for my red sedan but switch directions when two squad cars pull into the parking lot. I barely wait for the car to come to a complete stop before I'm pointing and giving directions for where they can find the killer.

When Logan gets out of the second vehicle, my heart skips a beat. We run towards each other, colliding in a hug that sets more tears loose. "Wesley's inside. He heard me talking about him, telling Marianne all I knew about the murder. He cut the power to try and get us."

Logan's hand cups the back of my head. His body is tense, but his voice is tender. "Are you hurt?"

"No. I don't think so."

Logan shifts me to his left so he can welcome Marianne to rest on his right side. "You're bleeding, Marianne. I'll call a medic."

I gasp as I turn to my best friend, only just now seeing her under proper light that shines through the parking lot. A gasp flings out of me when I see blood dripping down her lips and chin. "What happened?!"

Marianne hiccups through her pain and terror. "When we tripped over the stepstool, I bashed my nose on the edge of a shelf. I'm okay."

I release my grip on Logan and lower her to the asphalt. "Honey, let me look at it." I motion for Logan to go with the rest of the officers. "We left Wesley a few feet behind the circulation desk."

"Left him how?" Logan's mouth stiffens. "I was kind of hoping that you would have been able to avoid him until we got here."

"That was the plan, but we didn't have much of a choice. He might be trapped under a bookstack that we pushed over onto him when he was coming for us."

Logan's eyes widen. "Are you serious?"

I nod, casting around for anything that might stem the bloody flow of Marianne's nose.

Logan takes out his gun and holds it aimed at an angle toward the ground. "Stay right here." He stalks off to join the other officers, leaving us to hold tight to each other. "Here. This will help." It takes some doing, but I manage to rip off some stitching on my shoulder so I can tear off my sleeve altogether. I dab at Marianne's face with the cloth, and swipe at her tears with my thumb. "I'm so sorry this happened in your beautiful library. I'll help you clean up those books. We'll set it all right; like it never happened."

"But it did happen. Wesley Swanson murdered Jared." Marianne cries harder. No matter how quickly I wipe away her tears, more keep blooming, rolling down her high cheekbones.

I hold her tight with one arm and tend to her face with my free hand. We grip each other as we sit on the ground, watching the building with rapt focus, waiting for the door to open and Wesley to come out in cuffs.

"Please don't let him have escaped," I mutter, my fears getting the best of me.

It seems like an eternity passes before the front doors swing open. It's my turn to burst into tears when Logan and his partner come out of the building with Wesley in handcuffs, limping and barely upright.

We did it. We escaped and brought Jared's killer to justice.

Marianne sobs in my arms as relief spreads through us both. I had hoped that the killer didn't reside in Sweetwater Falls. I wanted so badly for there to be any other explanation. But as Wesley lowers his head in surrender, I know that Lisa's life is about to be forever changed.

Though I wish I could fix it all, I know that there aren't enough double fudge cupcakes in the world to make up for the fact that Lisa's husband is a murderer.

20

WINIFRED'S RENT

I don't know the best way to say, "I'm sorry your husband is a murderer. I still love you," but cupcakes seem to be able to communicate far better than I ever will with mere words. I'm not sure how many cupcakes it will take to bring Lisa back into society, but half a dozen a week seems like a good start.

Still, two weeks after Wesley's arrest, I haven't heard a peep from Lisa. I've suggested going over to deliver the cupcakes in person, but Winifred threw a blanket over that idea. "Give her time, dear. She knows it's not your fault. Let Agnes keep dropping off the cupcakes to her once a week. Agnes has a way about her that can put back together even the most damaged soul."

I sigh, knowing she's right. "Okay. I just hate that there's nothing I can do."

Marianne presses a kiss to my shoulder while she continues putting liners in the cupcake pan. The bruising on her face from bashing her nose during our escape from the library is gone, thankfully, but the memory of her wound still stings my heart.

Winifred opens the fridge and takes out a bottle of milk, pouring herself a glass. "Well, this isn't your wrong to right.

Wesley is the one who put Lisa in this position. You're being a good friend, and that's all you can do. The rest is up to Lisa. She gets to decide how long this is going to keep her down."

"You're right. Of course. Do you ever tire of carrying around this much wisdom?"

Winifred winks at me as she sits at the kitchen table. "Constantly. Not many are blessed with good looks and wisdom, but what can I say? When it rains, it pours." She fluffs her silver curls just to coax a giggle out of me. "Are you sure you girls don't want my help?" Winifred offers for the second time this morning.

I shake my head. "We've got a system."

Marianne holds up the cupcake liners. "A system and a trusty dishwasher on his way."

Winifred chuckles after finishing her glass of milk. "I trust my rent is going to be ready soon?"

I bump my hip to her shoulder while I whisk egg whites by hand. "Your cupcake with double the frosting is right there on the counter. I've decided whenever I'm doing mass orders like this one, you always get the first cupcake."

"As it should be."

When I offered to pay Aunt Winifred for managing the cupcake pickups and using her kitchen far more than either of us expected I would when I first moved in a few months ago, she laughed, assuming I was joking. "I'll not take a penny from you, honey cake. Keep feeding me cupcakes, and I'll be happy."

I took her words literally, making sure there is always a cupcake waiting for her when she finishes dinner, and two extras for Karen and Agnes.

Marianne takes the scoop and starts filling the cupcake liners two-thirds the way full. "I can't believe how many orders you have today. On top of the Sheriff's birthday party at the precinct, no less." She glances around the kitchen. "We've been at this for a few weeks now, and the orders are only increasing. Pretty soon we're going to outgrow this kitchen."

I love that she says "we" as if it's a given she will always be by my side, fighting for my business and making my passion come to life.

"I have to wait until I have a certain number in the bank and all my commercial supplies purchased before I think about expanding. Lisa's plan is perfect; I just have to be disciplined and follow it exactly. I don't want to let her down."

That's a laugh. I've already played a part in getting her husband locked up. I highly doubt that she would notice or care if I veered off course.

When the doorbell rings, I bring the bowl with me to let Logan in. "How is the best baker in Sweetwater Falls today?" he asks as he comes inside and slides off his shoes.

"A little behind, but other than that, I'm doing alright. How's the best police officer in Sweetwater Falls?" I keep whisking while I talk.

Logan frowns, one hand behind his back. "You didn't drop the bowl."

I glance at the egg whites and sugar, which have only formed soft peaks. They need a bit more air whipped in before they're done. "Was I supposed to? It's not heavy."

"Is that it? You're not clumsy around me anymore? Is the magic gone between us? I take you out, and that's that? I'm just regular old Logan to you now?"

I know he's joking, but I bump my hip to his all the same. "Never."

"Good. Then you can have this." He slides a single stem pink rose from behind his back. "Something pink in case nothing I do makes you blush."

His sweetness colors my cheeks, which spreads a smile across his handsome face. "Thank you."

Logan kisses my cheek, then walks beside me as we move into the kitchen. He leans over and pecks Winifred's cheek, and then hugs Marianne. "Have no fear, ladies, your dishwasher is here." He rolls up his sleeves and starts in on the mountain of dishes piled in the sink without being asked. "Good morning, Buttercream. Are the girls giving you any love today?"

My goldfish on the windowsill over the sink swims around in response.

Logan motions to my cactus. "It's looking good, Miss Charlotte. What's your secret?"

"I didn't water it, didn't touch it, and put it in the window for sunlight."

"Excellent plan. I guess I can stop feeding mine potato chips to see if it grows faster than yours."

I snicker at his antics. "You're not really giving your cactus potato chips."

"Well, not anymore, I'm not."

The three of us move around the kitchen easily now, and I love it. His flower goes into the tall, slender vase to join the stems he brought me the last time he came over, and the time before that. I love the look of the pop of nature smack in the middle of culinary heaven.

"How is your father holding up, Logan?" Winifred asks. "It's not easy getting older. Not that I would know."

Logan talks over the flow of the sink. "He's less than pleasant. I'm hoping the cupcakes I bring to the office to celebrate might cheer him up."

Winifred chuckles as she shakes her head. "That's the thing about life. You can't be afraid of it. You have to take it at a run, otherwise not even cupcakes will be able to get you through." She swipes her finger across the top of the cupcake I saved for her. "I don't think life would be worth the effort if cupcakes couldn't brighten your day."

"Hopefully Miss Charlotte's double fudge does the trick, otherwise he's going to be a pill to work with today."

"As opposed to his usual cheery self?" Marianne snickers as she slides a tray into the oven.

Winifred sucks the frosting off her finger. "It would be a shame if the sheriff didn't have something unexpected to brighten his day. Shake him out of his doom and gloom over getting one year older."

Logan shoots her a narrowed eye over his shoulder. "You wouldn't be planning anything devious, would you?"

"Who me? Never. I'm just a sweet little old lady. The birthday balloons filling the empty prison cell got there all by themselves."

Logan's eyes widen. "What? How did you manage that?"

Winifred chortles to herself. "Never you mind. You'll see them when you get there. Can't miss them, really. The real question is how did three little old ladies have the lungs to fill up two hundred balloons?"

Marianne and I don't say a thing. Our fingers are still sore from helping the Live Forever Club tie up the two hundred balloons last night. Logan doesn't need to know that Winifred has a key to the precinct. Winifred, Agnes and Karen used it to sneak into the police station last night and fill the jail cell with birthday balloons.

Logan also probably doesn't need to know that Winifred rigged each the sheriff's desk with small confetti bombs set to blow glitter at the man each time he opens one of his drawers.

He also would probably rather not hear about the picture of the sheriff's face that Karen taped onto the urinals in the bathroom at the precinct.

Marianne and I can claim plausible deniability to everything except for the balloons we helped them blow up and wrangle into their golf carts. We don't need any more attention from local law enforcement after giving our statements about Wesley's attack to the police.

Winifred didn't get home until two in the morning, but she doesn't look as if she's missed a minute of her required sleep. She smiles at her cupcake, taking a bite and closing her eyes as the flavors hit her tongue.

I love it here. I love living with my cooky great aunt. I love that she lets me pursue my passions and take up space in her world. I love that I have a best friend who will unleash her wild side to protect me.

And I love that I have my very own dishwasher who brings me roses and talks to my fish.

Most of all, I love Sweetwater Falls. For all of its flaws, this precious town welcomed me in and gave me the tools I needed to pursue my dreams...

...and the people to push me forward, holding my hand along the way.

LEAVE A REVIEW

Love the book?
Leave a review!

PUMPKIN SPICE SCARE

Pumpkin Spice Scare is book four in the Cupcake Crimes series.
Enjoy a free preview here:

Pumpkin Spice Scare

My stomach is in knots. I didn't sleep well last night, though, I'm not sure how well one is supposed to sleep in situations like this. I'm not a quitter, but today, that's exactly what I'm about to do.

When a knock sounds on my bedroom door, I finish pinning up my blonde waves. "Come on in, Aunt Winnie."

My sweet ninety-one-year-old great-aunt comes in, tiptoeing like she's trying to sneak into the room. "Charlotte, are you coming down to breakfast soon? I've got a surprise for you, and I'm no good with patience."

"A surprise?" I light up like a little girl on Christmas morning. "You didn't have to make a big fuss."

Aunt Winnie puts her hands on her hips, her silver curls swooshing across her shoulder. "Young lady, it's not every day a person quits their day job because their passion project turned into actual income. This deserves a celebration." True joy dances in her glassy sea-green eyes. She looks about ten seconds away from pulling out a camera so she can capture baby's first time quitting a job.

I grimace when I hear something crashing downstairs. "Was that part of the surprise?"

"It better not be. Those girls, I swear..." She marches out of my bedroom, leaving me to finish getting ready for my big conversation with my boss at Bill's Diner, in which I will inform him that I am quitting.

I hustle down the steps, nearly falling on my backside when the kitchen erupts with a joyous "Congratulations!"

How Agnes, Karen, Marianne and Fisher managed to stay so quiet that I didn't hear them come inside this morning is beyond me. In the next breath, I am scooped into hugs and cheek pinches as my closest friends in Sweetwater Falls make my celebration their own. The kitchen smells like ham, which makes my mouth water. I can tell Fisher was in charge of the food because it smells like pure love.

I adore these people. I can't get enough of this precious little small town. Moving here from a big city a few months ago was the best decision I've ever made—other than opening a cupcake bakery from Aunt Winnie's house.

I really didn't see that taking off, but after one short month, I have enough saved to be able to quit my day job and pursue baking cupcakes full-time. Or, I will in two weeks, which is why this morning I am putting in my two-week notice with Bill.

There goes that stomachache again. I don't want to let Bill down, but I think it's obvious that waitressing at his greasy spoon diner isn't my life's calling.

My best friend loops her arm through mine, her grin a mile wide. "I'm so excited for you! I barely slept last night. Are you beaming?" Marianne flips one of her two brown braids over her shoulder, motioning for me to sit at the round table in the corner of the kitchen.

"You know that feeling you get right before you go over the

edge of a roller coaster's big hill?" I motion to my stomach. "That's what I'm feeling. Happy and nauseous."

Fisher slides a plate of food onto the table while Marianne pulls out my chair for me. Fisher grins at my wide eyes as he pushes his black curls away from his round face. "What, you've never seen eggs benedict with a side of country ham before?"

"Not in this kitchen, no. You didn't have to go to all this trouble. I know you're busy at The Snuggle Inn."

Fisher waves off my concern. His hairy forearms are thick. They flex as he sets down silverware beside my plate. "And miss this? Nah. This is a big deal, Charlotte. You've been putting in a heap full of hours, working your day job plus trying to get your cupcake empire off the ground. I only wish I could be there when you tell old Bill you won't be his waitress anymore. He's been getting on my last nerve lately."

"Being his usual charming self?" I tease. My boss is the definition of grumpy.

"You know it." Fisher turns off the stove and slaps my hand. "I have to get back to work. Congratulations, Charlotte McKay. I want every detail of how sour Bill's face looks when you tell him his favorite waitress is quitting." He moves his fingers through his black curls. He's a good decade and a half older than I am, but when he is at work in a kitchen, he looks far younger.

My nose crinkles. "I'm hardly his favorite. Bill can't stand me." The feeling is mutual.

"Aw, that's just Bill's way. Good luck, kiddo." Fisher hugs Aunt Winnie on his way out, leaving me with the best breakfast in the world. Fisher's passion for food matches my obsession with cupcakes, so we understand each other well. Each bite of this meal is a treat. The fact that it was made just for me? I don't know how I got to be so spoiled.

Karen pours herself a glass of orange juice and sits across

from me with a half-eaten plate of the delicious breakfast. "No more talk of Bill. It's time for presents!" She surprises me by pulling out a small box and slapping it on the table. "It's from the Live Forever Club."

I glance up at Karen, Agnes and Aunt Winifred, wondering if there has ever been a more fantastic and adventurous group of women. "A present? You didn't have to do that."

Agnes tugs a second envelope from her pocket and sets it in front of Marianne. She straightens her shoulders and places her hand atop Marianne's head. "A gift for our junior members."

Marianne marvels at the three in similar fashion. "For me? But this is Charlotte's big day. I don't need a gift."

Aunt Winnie pinches Marianne's cheek. "If not for all the hours you put in, my Charlotte's dream would have taken a lot longer to come true. You're the one who pushed for this to happen. This is just as much your victory as it is Charlotte's."

I squeeze Marianne's hand, agreeing wholeheartedly. "You come over practically every other day after working at the library to help me bake. You're the one who helped me turn this into a business. They're right; you deserve whatever is in that envelope."

Marianne's caution turns to glee. "Shall we?"

Karen takes a sip of her juice. "If you don't open those things, I will."

I love these three wrinkled ladies who refuse to grow old. They're always up to something wild. "You didn't have to get me anything." The protest is weak, because I tear open the envelope with gusto, excited to get a gift. My mouth falls open when I pull out a certificate for...

I can't be reading this right.

"What is this? Aunt Winnie, did you seriously get us flying lessons?"

Marianne guffaws. "This is nice, but you know I'm afraid of heights."

Karen toasts us with her orange juice. "We sure do. Charlotte faced her fear of going into business for herself. You're next. There was a long waiting list, so those lessons won't actually happen until the spring. Plenty of time to gear yourself up for it."

Marianne looks like she might vomit. "You already booked it?"

Agnes grins, gleeful in her mischief. "We sure did. There's no backing out now."

Karen taps the edge of my gift certificate with her thin, knobby finger. "You've proved that you're Charlotte the Brave by opening the Bravery Bakery. And you've shown that you're Marianne the Wild by pushing through any resistance to make this happen. Since the sky is the limit with qualities like that, we figured you should start working on crashing any limits that the sky might have in store for you."

The poetic sentiment rings through my body, jerking my heart to the forefront.

Agnes kisses Marianne on the cheek, and then me. "Big life moments deserve to be commemorated." She holds onto Marianne's hand. "You can do it, Marianne. Then when the two of you fall in love with flying and get your pilot's license, you can fly us all over the place. We'll be world travelers."

I snicker at their grand plans and even grander imaginations. "So this is actually a gift for you, right?"

Agnes winks at me. "All the best ones are."

Though I've never set my sights on learning to fly, the prospect of someday learning sounds like a lot of fun—scary though it may be. "Thank you so much. I can't wait to give this a try." And I truly mean it.

"This is your moment, girls." Aunt Winnie postures, looking on us with pride. "Use it unwisely."

Marianne holds my hand under the table, no doubt just as spooked as I am that this is what constitutes an appropriate gift these days. I can tell that when the lessons near, Marianne is going to do her best to find a way out of this.

Which means it will be my job to make sure she gives it a try.

Aunt Winifred squeezes my shoulder. "Hurry up and finish eating, honey cake. That waitressing job isn't going to up and quit itself."

Karen leans her elbow on the counter. "I can't believe you're giving your two weeks instead of just quitting. At this rate, that halo of yours is never going to be tarnished." She tsks me, shaking her head as if I've missed the point of life.

I chuckle in her direction. "I have to go there anyway. I left my sweater there yesterday. Besides, I don't want to leave Bill in a lurch."

Winifred snickers into her morning tea. "My little rule follower. Whatever shall we do with you?"

It's an effort, but I manage to get myself out the door without being late for my shift. I have pink lipstick kiss marks on my left cheek from all the times Agnes kissed me, and red on my right cheek from the many times Aunt Winnie pinched me with her semi-arthritic grip.

The high of being sent off on this momentous day crests on the drive into work, and crashes completely when I get into the diner before it's opened to the public for the day. I hate letting people down, and I'm no good at confrontation.

I glance around the diner, noticing Judy's old brown clunker, Heather the hostess' silver coupe, the cook's mini-van and Bill's truck in the parking lot, along with my red sedan. Judy missed her shift yesterday, which put Bill in a bad mood. I'm glad she's here today, so Bill doesn't go off on a rant about responsibility before I can get a word in.

My steps are slow yet determined as I march into the diner in the early dawn light, my black apron tied around my waist and a no-nonsense look on my face. I greet the teenaged hostess, who pops her pink gum without looking up at me. Heather occupies herself by scribbling on a notepad with her headphones on, tuning out the rest of the world as she always does before the shift starts.

I don't see Judy, who usually spends her minutes before we open sitting in a booth in the corner, writing in a journal with unmitigated focus. I hope she's not chatting with Bill. I really need to talk to him before I lose my nerve.

I summon up my nerve and march into the kitchen, my voice louder than it should be. "Bill? Bill, I need to talk to you."

Bill is busy beside the line cook. He barely glances up when I speak. "If it's about asking for a raise, you can skip it. Heather and Judy both made their opinions clear in the past two weeks. If you get on my back about the pay, too, I might lose it."

I should probably learn how to interact with Bill without rolling my eyes, but the man has an uncanny knack of bringing out the teenager in me. "Could we talk in private? Like, sitting down?"

Bill squints at me. "We can talk exactly as we are. What's so important you have to slow down the morning prep, Charlotte?"

I envisioned quietly sitting in his office, explaining how grateful I am that he took a chance on me—a girl with no waitressing experience—giving me a job when I was new in town and needed someone to hire me. I have a speech prepared about ambition, complimenting him on his own and how it led him to run Bill's Diner. Then I planned to segue into telling him I am going to open my own cupcake bakery.

In my imagination, he is proud of me.

But that beautiful moment I imagined crumbles before my eyes when I blurt out an uncouth, "Bill, I'm putting in my two week's notice." My voice quiets as his knife stills. "If that's okay."

Bill narrows his eyes at me. "Two weeks?"

"Yes, sir. Thank you for..."

But I don't get out my gratitude before Bill waves off my words. "Fine, fine. Can you refill the ketchup bottles? Judy was supposed to do it yesterday, but she was a no-show. If she pulls that again this morning, I'll be out two waitresses."

Well, I guess there's no love lost between us. "Sure thing. I saw her car in the lot. I'll go get her, then I'll see to the ketchup. Thanks for everything, Bill."

And I truly mean it. I am grateful for this smelly, outdated place.

I am also grateful to be moving on.

I trot out to the dining area, glancing around to Judy's usual morning booth. "Heather, has Judy come in yet?"

Heather shrugs, her eyes still on her notepad. "I don't see her, so I guess not."

As employees, we are not an enthusiastic bunch. Poor Bill.

I can't believe I just quit. I actually did it. I worried last night when I had trouble falling asleep that I might chicken out. But I did it.

I was Charlotte the Brave.

And now I've got to tell Judy that she might have to handle more tables if Bill can't replace me in the next two weeks.

I check the women's bathroom and then decide to go back out into the parking lot. I like how the air feels in the morning before the sun has had its chance to do its best. The early October air has shifted to bring a slight chill, making me think my purple knitted sweater might not be enough to get me through the autumn season once it sets in more fully. I like how nature wakes me up, even if it leaves a chill on my skin.

My steps are quick as I jog out toward Judy's brown clunker, noting that the bumper is still askew. I didn't realize how useful duct tape could be; it's held her bumper on for at least as long as I've worked here.

I knock on Judy's window, donning a chipper smile. The glass is slightly fogged, but I see her outline in the driver's seat. She doesn't make to open the door, so I wait a few seconds, expecting some sort of response.

Maybe she's finishing up a phone call?

But there's no sound coming from inside the car.

After two more knocks, I worry she's fallen asleep. Poor thing. I wonder if she was a no-show yesterday because she was sick, and now she's come back to work too soon. She should go home and get some proper sleep.

I open her car door to tell her as much. "Judy? Hun, you should wake up. You'll catch a chill, napping in your car like this."

The sun isn't much help at the early morning, but the light from the inside of her car shines down, illuminating parts of her that still my words and steal my breath.

Pink, bubbly vomit has slicked and dried all down her front. Her lips are painted pink, but there is a discoloration around her mouth that infuses true fear in my soul.

"Judy?" My pulse quickens as I call her name in a whisper. "Judy! Judy, wake up!"

Her head lolls to the side, and for the first time, I realize her eyes are lidded but not closed.

Please let her be sleeping with her eyes open.

My fingers move slowly to her neck, feeling for a pulse, but nothing stirs beneath my fingertips.

My heart pounds so loud that I don't hear myself shouting her name over and over, even as I stumble back from her lifeless body. I grab my phone, dropping it twice before I take a picture of the scene and then call the police, hoping they will tell me that what I am seeing isn't what is real.

Judy made it to the parking lot, but she will never work another shift at Bill's Diner ever again.

Order *Pumpkin Spice Scare* today!

Sign up to get alerts for New Releases at
www.MollyMapleMysteries.com

DOUBLE FUDGE CUPCAKES

Yield: 12 cupcakes

From the cozy mystery novel *Double Fudge Felony* by Molly
Maple

*"I dump a fair drizzle of oil into the bowl, thinking that if I was
grieving and washing myself in guilt every day, I would want nothing
short of double fudge everything. Next comes some sugar, then a bit of
yogurt to give the chocolate flavor a little lift to it with a tang at the
end of each bite. I hum to myself as I set the mixer whirling."*

-*Double Fudge Felony*

Ingredients for the Cupcake:
   ¾ cups all-purpose flour
   ½ cup unsweetened cocoa powder
   1 tsp baking powder
   ½ tsp baking soda
   ½ tsp salt
   1/3 cup vegetable oil

½ cup granulated sugar

2 large eggs, room temperature

2 tsp pure vanilla extract

½ cup plain yogurt or vanilla yogurt, room temperature

Instructions for the Cupcake:

1. Preheat the oven to 350°F and line a cupcake pan with cupcake liners.
2. In a medium bowl, sift together ¾ cups flour, 1 tsp baking powder, ½ tsp baking soda, and ½ tsp salt. Set flour mix aside.
3. In a large bowl, use a mixer to beat the vegetable oil and sugar on medium speed for three minutes. Beat until shiny, scraping down the sides of the bowl as needed.
4. Add eggs one at a time while the mixer runs on low speed. Add 2 tsp pure vanilla extract. Mix until smooth.
5. With the mixer on low speed, add the flour mixture in thirds, alternating with the yogurt. Mix to incorporate with each addition, scraping down the sides of the bowl as needed. Beat until just combined. Batter should look a bit thin.
6. Divide the batter into your 12-count lined cupcake pan, filling each one 2/3 the way full.
7. Bake for 20-24 minutes at 350°F, or until a toothpick stuck in the center comes out clean.
8. Let them cool in the pan for 10 minutes, then transfer to a cooling rack. Cool to room temperature before frosting.

Ingredients for the Frosting:

4 oz. dark or semi-sweet chocolate

¾ cups unsalted butter

2 cups powdered sugar

2 Tbsp unsweetened cocoa powder

2 tsp pure vanilla extract

1½ tsp heavy cream (can substitute milk)

Flaked sea salt (optional)

Instructions for the Frosting:

1. Melt chocolate in the microwave in 30-second intervals, stirring in between until smooth. Set aside.
2. In your stand mixer, cut in the butter one tablespoon at a time, whipping until light and smooth.
3. Whip in cocoa powder, stirring down the sides until combined.
4. Add in powdered sugar one cup at a time, alternating with the vanilla and cream, stirring down sides of the bowl occasionally. Beat on high speed until frosting is soft and light, about 3-4 minutes.
5. Add in melted chocolate, whipping an additional 3 minutes until fluffy.
6. Optional step: top with a very light sprinkling of flaked sea salt.

ABOUT THE AUTHOR

Author Molly Maple believes in the magic of hot tea and the romance of rainy days.

She is a fan of all desserts, but cupcakes have a special place in her heart. Molly spends her days searching for fresh air, and her evenings reading in front of a fireplace.

Molly Maple is a pen name for USA Today bestselling fantasy author Mary E. Twomey, and contemporary romance author Tuesday Embers.

Visit her online at www.MollyMapleMysteries.com. Sign up for her newsletter to be alerted when her next new release is coming.

Made in the USA
Middletown, DE
12 February 2022

61047101R00102